A BUREAUCRATIC DESIRE FOR REVENGE

A COLLECTION

ANDREW DAVIE

Copyright (C) 2022 Andrew Davie

Layout design and Copyright (C) 2022 by Next Chapter

Published 2022 by Next Chapter

Edited by Tyler Colins

Cover art by Lordan June Pinote

Mass Market Paperback Edition

This book is a work of fiction. Names, characters, places, and incidents are the product of the author's imagination or are used fictitiously. Any resemblance to actual events, locales, or persons, living or dead, is purely coincidental.

All rights reserved. No part of this book may be reproduced or transmitted in any form or by any means, electronic or mechanical, including photocopying, recording, or by any information storage and retrieval system, without the author's permission.

For "Aunt" Carole

ACKNOWLEDGMENTS

Thank you Mike, Vince, Igor, Heather, Alec, Craig, John, Chris, Timothy, Cindy, Tyler, Miika, Petteri, and everyone at Next Chapter.

PUBLICATION HISTORY

Versions of these stories have appeared in:

Sissy Fish (Necessary Fiction)
Exit (Bristol Noir)
Custodian (Bristol Noir)
Escalation (Close to the Bone)
Forlorn Hope (Punk Noir Magazine)
...is machine... ill (Five:2:One)
Land of Some Other Order (Pulp Modern)
Nothing Good Happens Outside a Waffle House at 3 am. - (Lord Stanley's Mug in Close to the Bone)
Perennial (All Due Respect Books Anthology)
Primer (Pulp Modern)
Sometimes They Wouldn't Go Away (Close to the Bone)
The Bodysnatcher (Mystery Tribune)
The Golem (Bristol Noir)
The Treehouse (Yellow Mama)
With Gun, During Violence (Bristol Noir)
Failure Drill (Bristol Noir)
Three Little Pigs (Yellow Mama)

CONTENTS

Sissy Fish	1
Exit	10
Custodian	17
Escalation	25
Forlorn Hope	31
... is Machine ... ill ...	38
Land of Some Other Order	43
Nothing Good Ever Happened Outside of a Waffle House at 3 AM	47
Perennial	50
Primer	60
Sometimes They Wouldn't Go Away	63
The Bodysnatcher	69
The Golem	80
The Treehouse	87
With Gun, During Violence	93
Failure Drill	97
Three Little Pigs	103
Junk Paper	115
About the Author	134

SISSY FISH

The Job

Wake up hungover, either alone, living in a motel as a result of an impending divorce/trial separation (she kept the house), or next to a half-naked woman you've met/picked up/had sex with in the previous six hours (most, if not all, of which you can't remember).

When the beeper goes off a second time, hurl it against the opposite wall; this follows for both scenarios. If alone, throw up in the toilet/sink and stare at your reflection in the mirror. Don't say anything. Instead, display a fed-up grimace, the kind which exemplifies *I'm not angry, I'm just disappointed*. Change into work attire.

If alone, do a shnort of vodka (a mini bottle) before heading to the unmarked patrol car. If said half-naked woman is still asleep, suggest she can let herself out, and there's (possibly) pizza in the refrigerator. If half-naked woman is awake, listen to her make incredibly insightful remarks about the out-of-control state of your life, while she covers herself with the newly purchased minimal thread count sheets, then brush it off by saying something like, "I didn't know they were handing out Rhodes Scholarships with your tit job." Then, suggest there's pizza in the fridge. In this scenario, remove the mini bottle of vodka from the glove compartment, and shoot it on the way to, or upon arriving at, the crime scene.

The Dead Body

Walk into cordoned off apartment and greet officer Jones/Baxter (not Johnson, which would make him FBI, or Lynch which would make him CIA). Exchange pleasantries, accept coffee, and ask him who the lead detective is. Curse under your breath when you find out it's McDougall. Pinch the bridge of your nose and make reference to how McDougall couldn't find Joe Frazier in a bowl of rice.

Finish the coffee, walk the perimeter, and examine the scene. Lift the sheet off the body. Feel the adrenalin course through. Notice the vacant look in the eyes, and the lingering aura of dread which still circles the now empty vessel. Do *not* notice the white knuckles of your hand.

Place the sheet back. Go over the mental checklist for later: interview witness accounts, go over DNA findings, and NCIC reports. Try to exclude wrath/vengeance on the list of things to do. Put the sheet back and nod to Baxter/Jones. Leave the house and take a deep breath. Note the paradox: if you could quit the job, you would, but it's also the only thing keeping you going. Try and fail to block from your mind the fact the victim is around the same age as your son/daughter.

Old Habits are Like Bruce Willis

On the way home, deviate from the route. Pick up a baseball mitt/dress for son/daughter as a paltry excuse for missing their dance recital/play. Walk to the front door of your former dwelling and ring the bell. Feel the anger begin to build as you fondle the key in your pocket.

The door opens. Get chastised by soon to be/current ex-wife which begins with her saying, "You've got some nerve." Hold up the mitt/dress like a talisman, hoping it'll melt her icy demeanor. She laughs and aims to close the door in your face; block it from shutting with your foot. Say something witty/charming/insulting with usual rapier-like delivery. Cut to rolling around on living room floor with soon to be/current ex-wife who says, "Keep it down, you can't stay the night anymore; your son/daughter is getting confused."

Have angry/explosive attempt to remain quiet during sex. Try to kiss her goodbye at the doorway, but she dodges it. Settle for a halfhearted embrace. Drink another vodka mini in the car.

Through the Looking Glass

Visit with junkie/scumbag/informant. Slap him/her around a little and remind him/her about being able to bust him/her on a parole violation. Listen to him/her ask for some leniency/quarter before relenting. Allow him/her to fire up a pipe/smoke/joint or do a line to soothe nerves. Commiserate about what constitutes a difficult life for the appropriate amount of time.

Ask each other about your respective kids. Listen to a surprisingly coherent rant about choices/regrets/soul-searching, and quotations from Aristotle/Gandhi/Malcolm X/Timothy Leary. Receive information about a suspect in the case you're working. Give the informant/junky/philosopher a ten/twenty and tell him/her to keep his/her finger on the pulse. Get into the car and pity him/her for being an addict. Search through the empties in the glove compartment for a shnort of vodka.

The Watering Hole

Order a shot of Jameson's with a beer chaser. Tell the bartender to stick it he knows where when he says your tab is getting higher than a current/former rock star with drug problem/recent overdose/rehab stint/death. Sit at the bar with Sgt. Jones/Baxter, clink shots together, and drink them. Kill the beer and order another round. Listen to "Revelations" by Iron Maiden on the Jukebox, which only has three working CDs: Journey's Greatest Hits, Maiden, and Smooth Sounds of the Seventies, Volume 4.

Scope the bar for a potential sexual partner. Order another beer and feel the sensation of euphoria reach its apex. Scowl openly when McDougall walks into the bar. Mock his voice and mannerisms to Baxter/Jones, who suggests you're saying everything louder than you think you are, so you might want to keep it down. Ignore him and begin disparaging McDougall, who finally recognizes and grants you an audience. Exchange barbs with him until a group tries and fails to separate the two of you.

Go outside, shadowbox for a few seconds, almost

fall down from being inebriated, but manage to play it off. Miss with the first two punches as McDougall says to go sleep it off. Get more angry at the fact he's sober and condescending to you. Catch him with a leaping straight right. Watch as he transforms from playful/annoyed to murderous.

Absorb three punches and before going down, remember McDougall was a Gold Gloves boxer in his youth. Hear what sounds like Charlie Brown's teacher lecture you on how you are a good cop but disappoint everyone. Get helped to your feet by Baxter/Jones, who agrees to drive you home.

Beyond the Wall of Sleep

Wake up hungover on the front lawn, arms wrapped around a garden gnome named Pickle Bottom. Retch, but make it to the sink/toilet in the house after fumbling for the keys for what feels like an eternity. Fill the bowl with the remnants of last night. Stare at the face in the mirror with an eye that resembles a ripe plum and is almost closed completely. Almost laugh when you realize the hieroglyphics above your right eyelid are from McDougall's ring, Class of '91, in reverse.

Remove ice from the freezer and apply it to the bruised area. Wince from the pain. After twenty minutes, take a hot shower, shut the blinds, and get into bed to sleep off the hangover. Right before you shut your eyes, remember you were supposed to have breakfast with your son/daughter two hours earlier.

ANDREW DAVIE

Comeuppance

Wait outside the bar/restaurant/stomping ground where the suspect spends his time. Take a slow pull of the pint to ease the tension/anticipation/nerves/anger. Watch the suspect leave. Follow him at a distance, and park far enough away from his house so no one will remember your car/notice your presence/write down the license plate. Remove the throwaway piece from the glove compartment and chamber a round. Walk toward the door of the suspect's apartment with blinders on, incapable of processing any sense except sight.

Check the mailboxes for the apartment number and ride the elevator to the apartment. Wait outside the doorway and gather your thoughts. Ignore the smell of urine, and the sound of television programs from neighboring apartments. Remember the frozen grimace on the victim's face. Remind yourself he/she was your son's/daughter's age.

Press the doorbell. Keep your finger on the peephole. Hear footsteps approach. Clench your fist around the butt of your weapon. Hear the suspect ask, "Who it is?" Respond with, "The Super."

Hear the bolt unfasten. Kick the door in and hit the suspect in the face with the butt of the throwaway. Hear his nose break. Feel temporary delight. Shut the door behind you. Point the throwaway at the suspect. Watch his confusion turn to fear. Click off the safety with your thumb.

Remember the look on the victim's face. Slowly squeeze the trigger. Anticipate the spray of bone, brain, and blood, the smell of cordite, the sudden illumination of the muzzle flash, the kick of the gun, and the satisfaction. Don't pull the trigger. Lower the gun. Feel the tears stream down your face. Have an epiphany about your son/daughter.

Handcuff the suspect and Mirandize him. Experience a sensation which comes with doing the right thing long thought dormant or dead.

The Piper at the Gates of Dawn

Take a deep breath while outside the house. Anticipate the building rage, but find it's replaced instead by longing. Fondle the key in the pocket and debate using it, but refrain. Become overwhelmed by the desire to set things right, make amends for past transgressions, become a better father, rectify problems with the marriage, and enforce the law while on the job.

Press the bell and wait. Hear the footsteps growing louder until the soon to be/current ex opens the door. Implore her to listen before she begins to berate you, and for some reason she does. Maybe there's something in the tone of your voice or the look on your face. Find her staring at the contusion with concern and assure her you're okay.

You're certain she'll stop you from entering, or at least she'll hesitate, but she allows you into the house and guides you over to the couch. She says she'll get you some coffee. Feel the warm sensation of guilt consume you. Begin to cry, fight against it, and succeed in keeping it muffled. Understand, for the first time clearly, your former life is what you desire more than anything. Resign yourself to do whatever it takes to reconstruct the fractured pieces. Dedicate all free time to being an integral part of your son/daughter's life.

Walk over to the bookshelves and grab a Kleenex. Find the book of Greek myths you'd purchased and read together with your son/daughter, and how he/she had trouble pronouncing Sisyphus's name. Remember how you avoided mentioning the punishment Sisyphus endured and how the concept of eternity seemed incomprehensible, even to you. Promise to forsake the bottle, look up substance-abuse meetings in the area, and exercise more. Put in for a transfer from Homicide, make amends with McDougall, and recommend Baxter/Jones take the Sergeant's exam.

Take a deep breath and realize it no longer matters what set you adrift from the desired course you'd hoped your life would take. There's still time to right the ship, to make up for lost time, to become a person of substance, and to care about others more than you care about yourself. The feeling of satisfaction replaces the earlier guilt and melts away the shame, which up till now was threatening to consume you.

Sink back into the sofa cushions, which reminds you of the hours spent watching television with your son/daughter, of the countless hours falling asleep together with your soon to be reconciled/ex-wife, how you'd carry her up the stairs to the bedroom and kiss her on the forehead. Remember the warmth of her embrace. Smile at the thought, let your eyes wander around the living room, and settle on photographs of your children. Almost pass over the shiny object on the end table underneath the lamp. Furrow your brow as you begin to make out more details, and then get blindsided by rage when you *finally* comprehend why McDougall's class ring is there.

Falling Off the Edge of the World

Wake up hungover, and alone, living in a motel as a result of a divorce. Wait for the beeper to go off and remember you no longer have one. Take a hit from the pint of vodka on the nightstand. Lose track of which day it is. Take another hit from the pint and spill it on the end table. Use the recently opened court document as a coaster. Watch the dampness spread along the paper, which blurs your ex-wife's name, as well as the words: assigning, full, and custody. Finally, drag your body out of bed and walk toward the bathroom. Resemble the diagram on the museum wall depicting the evolution of Cro-Magnon man. Flip on the light switch and squint as the rods and cones trade places. Stare at yourself in the mirror with a look that suggests you're not angry, just disappointed. Wish, somehow, it wasn't all so predictable.

EXIT

Harry Gottlieb had never fired his weapon on the job; he'd never even drawn it off the range. That was fine. He could go to his grave without having gotten into a showdown. He'd known a few cowboys who'd needed to be the first through the door. They could keep it. Thankfully, as a transit cop, he rarely got into those situations. Only a few more years to go before he could put in for his pension and retire on half-pay. He'd go somewhere tropical where the weather was rarely
bad and the temperature never dropped below seventy.

On occasion, he would allow himself to indulge this fantasy, and then he would remember the outstanding debts he still had, including alimony. His dream of retiring with ease to the tropics would unravel. So, he forbade himself from thinking about it. Some might have been optimistic about the future, but Harry was more of a realist.

The other day, he collared a turnstile jumper; the man had a few priors, so a judge signed off on a search warrant. During a routine search of the man's apartment, they discovered hundreds of hours of film footage, all of it neatly categorized and time-stamped under file names too provocative and obscene to print. Most of the films were fetish specialties licensed to voyeuristic websites that specialized in subjects that didn't know they were being filmed. For a lighter sentence, the guy agreed to testify against the whole network: the filmmakers, the distributors, etc.

Did Harry get any recognition? As soon as the DA smelled something newsworthy, a special unit took over. "Thanks, Harry, we'll take it from here." The only way he was able to keep up with everything was due to a clerical error that kept him cc'ed on internal memorandums.

The door opened on the third knock but only a few inches as the chain was still affixed. Harry already had his badge out and held it up so she could see it.

"Diane Selnick?" Harry asked.

"Yeah."

"Now, what's the problem, officer?" It was almost as if she'd been resigned to getting busted for something eventually.

"I'm Harry." Not Officer Gottlieb. Put her at ease. "Can we speak inside for a minute?" he added.

She nodded, shut the door, and he heard the rattle of the chain coming undone. She opened the door and he walked inside. The TV was on, which she muted. There was a coffee table with a few magazines, a couch, and a cushioned chair. Nothing in the apartment matched. The walls had been painted off-white. There were a few bookcases stacked with classics and operating systems manuals.

Harry remained standing. He told her about the collar the other day. The guy's name was Randy Zwiebel. She didn't recognize it, but Harry put up his hand to suggest she just keep listening.

Randy had already cut a deal and couldn't give up names fast enough. Diane had been on the list as a webmaster of one of the sites in question. Harry told her he wasn't here to pick her up on anything; he could see to it her name was taken off the list.

"What would I have to do?" How she said it was monotone.

Harry got the sense that for a wizard with computers, her social skills were lacking.

"Don't worry," Harry said, "It's nothing like that."

He'd done some research on her. He knew which subjects to avoid. It would have been a mistake to mention alimony since she'd been part of a bitter custody battle as a kid, so he made certain not to bring that up. He knew she was looking for validation. So, instead, he was straight with her about his desire to finally enjoy life after putting in so much unrecognized work at his job. As a webmaster and coder, he knew she never got the spotlight.

Whether or not his reason had worked, she said she would hear him out. He explained what he had in mind, and if she joined, he would strike her name from the record. He also suggested if she turned him down and somehow came out of this thing unscathed, he could make life difficult for her.

She agreed to help him.

A BUREAUCRATIC DESIRE FOR REVENGE

He'd only ever come across penny shaving in fiction—rounding to the nearest cent during a financial transaction and putting the fraction into a separate account. Some had managed to use the method at gas pumps or, in one case, stealing almost $200,000 in coins from fareboxes over a few years. Both criminals had been caught.

With MetroCards, the fee was automatically deducted at the turnstile. What if there was a way to divert fractions of a penny of each transaction into a separate account? The trick would be getting away with it.

Diane told him she could write a program that would destroy itself after completing the final sequence. The only thing she needed was access to the servers. If he could get her that, the rest was pretty simple. He could do that. If they skimmed a penny at a time from the daily commuters at Union Square, they might get close to one and a half million dollars at the end of two years. The most difficult thing after the installation would be the waiting. It wasn't like winning the lottery, but if he was careful, he could make it last.

Diane had even agreed to take a lesser percentage since she had owed him for keeping her name out of the investigation. Almost everyone being prosecuted was going to stand trial and looking at possibly doing time.

The day of the installation arrived and everything went without a hitch. Harry had created an ID badge for her and if anyone asked, she was to tell them she was a new IT hire. No one asked; whether anyone even noticed she was there remained to be seen. Beforehand, she had explained to him what she was going to do, but it all sounded like a foreign language. Afterward, she told him unless someone was looking for it, the program would be difficult to find.

Now, all they had to do was wait. They both had access to the bank account, so they could check it. After the first fifteen hundred dollars was deposited, he asked her if she wanted to celebrate, just something lowkey, like one drink.

The drink became a monthly thing. On the fifteenth, every month, they would meet at Harry's apartment and have a screwdriver, easy on the orange juice. Over a year, they had accumulated almost eight hundred thousand dollars. Harry hadn't changed his lifestyle. He still cut the checks to Marie every month, griped about the job slowly eroding his will to live, and went bowling with Chavez and Moran when it was league night. However, he also resurrected his dream of escaping to paradise.

This time, he would fully indulge in the fantasy. He'd imagine himself lying in a hammock, swaying in the breeze, and drinking something with an umbrella served in a coconut husk. If he was frugal, he could make it last. Often, he thought about how Marie would respond when that first check didn't arrive. He would be gone, disappeared from existence. Throughout the year, he had slowly begun to remove himself from the grid, so when the time came, he'd be impossible to trace. At the year and a half mark, he'd start to make the withdrawals in increments to avoid detection as well. No matter what, he wouldn't let himself imagine the hammer dropping on his fantasy, not this time.

At the end of a year, Diane showed up at his house for their monthly drink with a suitcase.

"Going somewhere?"

"My mother's ill; I'm going to stay with her for a few weeks." She handed him a slip of paper. "Here's my contact info," she said.

He took the paper, crumpled it, and put it in his pocket. "Next time, you should clear this with me first," he said.

"There's not going to be a next time," she said, and her tone had changed. The hangdog look she always had now been replaced with fierce determination.

Harry tried to reply, but the words came out garbled.

"Have a seat," she said. She took his arm and led him over to his recliner.

He sat down. His head had begun to swim, and his stomach distended. She took out her phone, typed in a few things, and showed him the screen. Their bank account had a balance of zero.

"I've been spiking your drinks the last few months. The paper you put in your pocket had been dusted with powder. By itself, it's harmless, but the combination with what's already in your system is lethal. Don't worry, I planted a draft of a suicide note in your outgoing email."

She started toward the door.

He tried to speak, but again the words wouldn't

come. When he tried to stand, he fell out of the chair and onto the floor.

"It took a while to copy your style, but I think I got it in the end. I just felt it was fair you should know. Don't worry. I'll probably head somewhere tropical," she said casually.

CUSTODIAN

The man in question had been photographed placing the plastic explosive outside of Gribi's Bar & Grill at 2:00 a.m. The upstairs was a boarding house that still rented rooms. The explosion the following evening destroyed most of the establishment, killed a tenant, the bartender, and two of the waitstaff. The place hadn't yet started serving dinner or drinks for the after-work crowd, so no other patrons were harmed.

Unfortunately, debris from the explosion had put Rachel in the hospital. She had been walking toward her car and needed to pass in front of the restaurant. Soon after I'd heard the news and learned she was in the operating room, I found myself in Rick's office. Paul was there as well.

Rick Mikos's office was austere. Only the bare necessities: a desk, guest chair, couch, phone. No computer, no bar, no plants. He had a window, but the blinds were shut. Rick always had a permanent five o'clock shadow that had a bluish tint, even if he had shaved a few hours earlier. He also exclusively wore navy-blue suits. The only indulgence he allowed was a replica Winchester repeating rifle that hung on the wall behind his desk. He told me of its significance after I'd first started working for him and Paul, but I've since forgotten.

Paul Kraljević was the polar opposite. His office had every amenity invented: flat-screen television, wet bar, stereo system. He looked like Slim Jim Phantom from The Stray Cats and embraced the look: coiffed pompadour and sharkskin suit. Together, he and Rick seemed more like an 80s New Wave band than the syndicate which ran Fernley, Nevada.

"Had you set a date?" Rick asked.

Out of the corner of my eye, I saw Paul wince. Over the years, I'd learned Rick was blunt, but he was also empathetic.

"Rachel wanted June of next year," I said. The words sounded strange coming out of my mouth now.

"When are you going to head over to the hospital?" Paul asked.

"In a minute."

None of us spoke for another moment.

"What's the word on this guy?" I said and held up the grainy black-and-white from security footage. Rick and Paul had some legitimate people in law enforcement on the payroll and due to the sheer audacity of the bombing, as well as Rachel's involvement, the matter became a top priority.

Rick looked at a printout on his desk. The man in question went by the name of McQuaid. He worked freelance mostly. He had worn a ski mask, but there had been a gap between a glove and shirt sleeve that revealed a tattoo. After a few minutes of scrutinizing the photo, the NCIC was able to secure McQuaid's resume from Interpol. McQuaid had worked all over the world for both paramilitary organizations and terrorist groups. They were interchangeable, depending on semantics. Of course, it would also account for McQuaid's use of Semtex, and his ability to have acquired it in the first place.

I killed the rest of my drink. "That it?" I asked.

Rick and Paul exchanged glances. Paul went on to tell me McQuaid had almost certainly fled the United States for parts unknown, and he would be virtually impossible to trace. Every law enforcement acronym had a file on this guy and had been looking for him for the last five years. However, he and Rick had learned who had hired McQuaid and, based on the change of their demeanors, I could tell this was where the situation would get tricky.

"Vinnie Minthis," Paul said.

I digested the information and sat back in my chair.

Both Paul and Rick had been looking to expand their empire. Even though they were close to Reno, there was a whole world out there. Vinnie Minthis was a representative from an outfit back East who'd been sent to Reno as an intermediary to conduct business with Paul and Rick, as well as some other players on the West Coast. I'd only had a few interactions with Minthis, but it was enough.

"What are you thinking?" Rick asked me.

I had tried to keep my emotions in check, but Rick was a master at detecting subtle changes, so he recognized that fury had begun to build.

"Go to the hospital, then check with Olmstead ... see where he stands on all of this," I replied.

"Get some rest," Paul suggested. "We'll let you know what else we find."

I nodded and left my empty glass on the desk.

ANDREW DAVIE

Rachel was still in surgery when I got to the hospital. The on-duty nurse said they would let me know when she was out, but it wouldn't be for another few hours at least. I caught up with Rachel's brother Evan, who still lived in Fernley. I thanked the staff, told Evan I'd return, and went to see Olmstead.

Calvin Olmstead was a teetotaler who quoted scripture. He had an encyclopedic knowledge of the history of the area and would often go on tangents about the law of the Old West. As a judge, he was swift to dole out punishment. Leniency was unheard of for even minor infractions. However, the townsfolk of Fernley, NV had desired order above everything else, so while a few might have griped about it, most were content to sing his praises, especially since the temptation of Reno was only a half an hour away. He often ran unopposed for election.

I told him of the identity of McQuaid, and the suspicion McQuaid had been hired by Minthis. Olmstead wasn't fond of Minthis either, but Reno was out of his jurisdiction, and Olmstead told me until there was concrete evidence, it was hearsay. When I told him I disagreed with him, Olmstead's eyes blazed. His fine white beard and sunbaked scalp gave him the appearance of one of the biblical figures he often quoted.

"Justice will be served," he affirmed.

Olmstead eased back into his chair and his eyes kept their intensity. "Ed," he began, and took a deep breath. His tone softened. "I realize wrath is the only thing you're thinking of at this moment and the good Lord knows that I understand. However, 'Make sure nobody pays back wrong for wrong. Thessalonians, 5:15'."

He waited for me to answer. His library was lined with ornate bookcases and leatherbound volumes of mostly history. The stillness in the room was punctuated by the ticking of his grandfather clock. A maid appeared, carrying a silver tray with a teapot, cups, and sugar. Olmstead offered and I declined. I had the urge to reach for my flask, but knowing his aversion to alcohol, I refrained. He took a sip of his tea and held the cup and saucer in his well-manicured hands.

"This man, McQuaid, *will* stand trial in my court."

I finally replied by producing my flask and taking a long pull.

He processed the look on my face and decided to drop the pretenses. "I will charge you with contempt," he said. "For starters."

Olmstead didn't issue threats lightly, and I knew I was pushing it. So, I put the flask away. He was aware of my business in Fernley, and he tolerated Kraljević, Mikos, and me by extension, since we conducted ourselves as professionals, didn't violate his code of ethics, and stayed off his radar. Most importantly, we also kept the undesirable element from setting up shop in town. However, Olmstead could just as easily make things difficult and suggest bringing in a special prosecutor to Fernley.

"OK, your honor," I said and stood.

"Thank you."

I exited his study and finished the rest of the flask in the hallway.

When I returned, both Rick and Paul were in Paul's office. The flatscreen was muted, but the local newscasters were running a piece about the explosion with video coverage of the aftermath, and the planned restoration of the area. I told them about my conversation with Olmstead and a lack of resolution. McQuaid was in the wind and Minthis was above the law.

My cell phone rang. It was Rachel's brother Evan. He sounded like he had been hysterical, but had calmed down. It still took him a moment to tell me Rachel was dead. I thanked Evan, told him I would check on him later, and hung up the phone.

"She's dead," I said.

"Ed," Rick began, and Paul finished his thought.

"Nothing can come back to us."

I assured them it wouldn't.

Reno was a little less than forty minutes away and I got there in about half an hour. Vinnie Minthis had been looking for a home but, for the moment, still had a room at the Majestic Grand Resort and Casino.

I had called ahead under the pretense of business and was told I could get ten minutes. Minthis greeted me at the door. He'd just showered but still looked like he'd been lacquered. He wore a bathrobe bearing the hotel's insignia. I followed him inside.

"Drink?" he asked.

"Scotch," I replied.

The Presidential Suite was enormous, enough for at least four people, a view of downtown Reno, and top-of-the-line everything. Minthis began pouring drinks. However, after he set out the glasses, he took a comb from his pocket and went through his hair again.

"Sorry, this has to be short," he said and poured the drinks. "I've got dinner at a place supposed to have the best Eggplant Parm west of New Jersey."

I took a seat in one of the chairs by the coffee table. It was some sort of space-age velour that molded to my body.

Minthis handed me my drink and took a seat on the couch. "So," he began, "what can I do for Fernley?" He rested back on the couch and took a sip.

The pleasant look on his face disappeared when I produced the .38. He furrowed his brow as if he didn't understand. I had expected a tirade from Minthis, or at least the question of whether I was insane, but he stayed silent. However, the look of incomprehension remained.

"Silas Jackson had been a dealer at this casino before he became an informant for the FBI."

The look of confusion left Minthis's face.

"He'd rented a room above Gribi's Bar & Grill, and was going to meet with his handler at a satellite office in Carson City." I took a sip of my drink.

Minthis relaxed more.

"But you knew all of this," I said.

He nodded slowly. "And?" he asked. By now, all of the confusion was gone and he felt like he was in control again.

"And you figured why not take the gloves off in Fernley; as long as Jackson is taken out, who cares about collateral damage?" This time, I opened the briefcase and took out the rope.

He went back to looking confused.

"There's a guy I know," I began. "Judge Olmstead

knows everything about the ways of the Old West. Told me once about a 'custodian', someone who puts up bail money and could be sentenced in the accuser's place."

While I never gave Minthis credit for being that sharp, he finally seemed to get it.

"Now," I continued, "since Mr. McQuaid has disappeared, it looks like *you're* going to have to swing in his place."

ESCALATION

"Open the door," The Green Monster says. Standing a shade over five foot six, he borders on comedic with the incongruity of his appearance and threatening delivery.

"I can't do that right now, Dave," I say and wonder if he'll get the reference to film 2001. I sink further into the outline of his imprint in the material of the driver's seat of his BMW M3.

He tries the door handle again. It's like watching a wild animal on safari. I can smell the new car fragrance, but sadly no pine-cone air freshener dangles from the rearview mirror.

"Open the fucking door," he reiterates. He pauses between each word.

"Tell you what, Dave. I'll open the door when 'Dawning of the Knuckle Duster' finishes." I hit play on my iPod, which I've hooked up to the Bose speaker system he'd recently had installed, and music fills the car. "It's one song, and right now you've got thirty-three more minutes."

The Green Monster tries a different tactic. "Look,

this is funny, I get it. Watch me squirm a little, pull one over on the boss."

He sucks his teeth and places his hand back on the door handle, ready to get his way as he always does. "Now, open the door."

David Green, aka The Green Monster, earner of six million dollars last year, owner of an eight-bedroom house in Cos Cob, vacation home on the North Fork, this, and two other automobiles of equal or greater value, turns a maroon color, and the vein, subject of much mockery amongst the junior brokers, protrudes on his forehead.

I shut my eyes and ignore the fury of epithets and profanity-laced tirade which flow freely from The Green Monster's mouth at machine-gun staccato. The car begins to gather a small crowd of people.

"If I'm late for this meeting ..." The Green Monster bellows. He sprays the window with saliva, grips the handle, and pulls repeatedly.

The Green Monster is one of the most successful sales traders on Wall Street.

"Wall Street is an example of metonymy," I say. "It's both a place but can be substituted to mean a category of business."

The Green Monster has gone to Defcon 4. I've only seen him at Defcon 5 once.

His clients are big institutional firms or hedge funds who routinely buy and sell large block shares of stock worth millions of dollars. The Green Monster specializes in finding people to buy most or all his clients' shares so the stock price isn't affected. If we don't leave in three minutes—i.e., be on the road, make tracks, peel rubber—then he will be late to his meeting, pissing off, upsetting, shunning, slapping the collective faces of his biggest client.

The song starts to build to a crescendo, which won't truly crest for another twenty minutes.

The Green Monster loosens his tie. I can see him mulling over the various options of what to do: call a car service, cancel or postpone his meeting. In a manner more befitting a silverback gorilla, he raises the phone in the universal sign of trying to get a signal. He makes two more attempts, then the rage bursts forth, culminating in a yell which mirrors a war cry Genghis Khan may have used before he pillaged. It's loud and abrasive enough to draw stares from everyone in a one-block vicinity. The force of his kick is enough to shake the car's frame and puts a two-inch dent into the door.

"You're going to break your foot if you keep doing that."

"You're fucking fired, do you hear me!"

He kicks the door again. This time the people, who until now have kept their distance, begin to inch closer. After the fourth kick, The Green Monster loses steam and sags against the door. He stares at me, and his breath fogs the window.

"It's sort of like Schrödinger's Cat," I say.

"Why are you doing this?" he asks. This time, his voice lacks the usual snap.

I pause the song and, for a brief moment, the world is silent.

"Carbon Dioxide, CO_2, is one of the necessary components to life. Carbon monoxide is deadly. One oxygen atom separates them."

The Monster tries to open the door, hoping, maybe willing it to break from its hermetically sealed vacuum. The crowd is less interested than before, and a police officer stands at the fray, keeping a close eye, probably choosing not to intercede yet, so he won't have to fill out additional paperwork. He remains poised, though, ready to retrieve his nightstick, pepper spray, or firearm from its holster.

"What the fuck are you talking about?" The Monster demands. Slight twinges of fear begin to coat the anger in his voice.

"How can someone so good at making money be so ignorant about everything else?" I ask.

The Green Monster's mouth opens, but he doesn't say anything. He continues to back away from the car like it's a dirty bomb that has been activated.

"See, what we had before was called deterrence ... when two powers of equal strength are at an impasse. But now, well, I've sort of taken over, haven't I?" I state.

"H-hey, hey, hey," he stammers, repeating the words like if he says them enough, it will snap me back to a reality he can deal with.

Dave Green, aka The Green Monster, suddenly breaks down in an infantile manner where words make no coherent sense. He lurches his body onto the car. His palms smack the glass, and he resembles the slain carcass of a deer. He brings down his fists and wails. This time, he creates a hairline fracture in the windshield.

The police officer double times it over to the car, his left hand is outstretched and his right hand hovers a few inches away from his standard issue. "Sir, please step away from the vehicle."

"I'd do what he says, Dave. The last thing you'd

want to happen is blue suicide; I mean, how would you try to explain your tardiness to your clients then?"

The police officer steps around the hood of the car. "Sir, I want you to take your hands off the vehicle and take two steps back." The officer has now extended the pointer finger of his left hand. His right hand remains poised, a hooded cobra, ready to draw forth his weapon, click the safety, and fire.

The Green Monster continues to slam his fists onto the car. The crowd has completely circled the car and cell phones have been produced. It resembles a scene at an outdoor concert. This will no doubt become a viral sensation on the internet.

"Hey, Hulk, stop fucking around and do what he says," I suggest.

The cop has executed a textbook shooting stance. His corded muscles are taut; a Mozambique drill is only a moment away.

"That's also known as a failure drill or failure to stop the drill, where he'll put two in your chest and one in your head," I advise.

The Green Monster lifts his head and notices the officer, but his recognition of the authority wielded by this man, or the threat of death, has not broken Dave from his fugue state. His hands are riddled with tiny slivers of glass, which make them crystal geodes. The bashing continues, and the top section of the windshield loosens from its frame.

"Dave! Get the fuck away from the car!"

Dave's mouth purses to say something, and he's tasered with an X26, state-of-the-art device. The electrodes attach themselves to The Green Monster's neck, and he wriggles involuntarily. After a moment, he pitches forward, rolls off the hood of the car, and onto the ground.

The police officer continues to pump electrical current until he's certain The Green Monster is down for good. Some in the crowd cheer, others boo and make vacant proclamations about police brutality. Dave is hoisted to his feet by the police officer, who bends him over the hood, cuffs his hands behind his back, and Mirandizes him.

The Green Monster stares at me through the one unbroken part of the windshield. He blinks repeatedly to remove the dried blood from his eyes. I shut mine, hoping this vision won't be an after-image in my dreams.

FORLORN HOPE

"You do realize if you are apprehended, I will disavow this conversation ever took place," Tuttle had said.

"Scuse me?" Maynard had said.

"If they catch you, I won't know you."

J. Lawrence Tuttle had worn a gray suit that looked like it had been new off the rack. His face had been clean-shaven and had a pinkish hue. His black hair was neatly parted, and a watch chain led from his breast pocket to his vest button.

Elias Maynard's suit had long since started to come apart at the seams. He hadn't shaved in a few days, and he knew he probably smelled something foul. Although, by now, he had gotten used to it. Maynard glanced up and saw a framed diploma from Harvard Law School. It made sense. Tuttle wouldn't forgo the opportunity to display his pedigree. The rest of the office was immaculately clean. All the books were in alignment, and a grandfather clock ticked in the corner. Tuttle must have had a thing for timepieces.

Tuttle's suit and the office itself seemed out of

place for the times, though. Most of those items could have been sold to avoid the breadlines, but Maynard imagined Tuttle was steadfast about keeping up appearances. Tuttle had also seemed like the kind of person who loved the sound of his own voice, so it didn't surprise Maynard that he had to sit through a lecture.

It began with the birth of the motion picture industry and went on tangents. Tuttle defined positions on the set, who was responsible for what, and various steps and processes in which a film was made. Each time Tuttle wound down, something would spark another thought, and he'd sit back up in his chair, fully animated.

Maynard had replayed the conversation over again in his head, now, as he watched Piggy and Fluffy take in a jazz concert in the cartoon *You Don't Know What You're Doin'!*. The theater had been packed but Clem had been easy to spot in the darkness. Seated next to Maynard, Clem shoved another handful of popcorn into his mouth and chewed unmercifully. Maynard had already assured Clem they could get another bag if the vendor was still outside. Clem sat enamored, even though he had seen the cartoon at least five times in as many days. Around them was the raucous laughter of children.

Clem was probably blocking the view of everyone a few rows in back of him, but no one had approached the behemoth. Even though he was what they called shell-shocked, at 6'7" Clem was a force to be reckoned with. Nearly as wide as he was tall, he'd been fired from labor jobs for not knowing his own strength and destroying what had been referred to as "irreplaceable equipment". Clem had kicked around for a while, like a rudderless ship on the ocean, until he had hooked up with Maynard.

Maynard had recognized Clem's potential.

Maynard himself had been a rigger turned spotlight operator in the theater union, hanging lights for Vaudeville and magic acts like Chao Kong Moon. Before that, Maynard had tried his hand at a few different schemes. When those failed, he participated in a final gambit: a marathon dancing contest with Loretta. When things had been at their worst, Maynard always had Loretta. Even when he had humiliated himself to make an extra cent, she still loved him unconditionally.

The dance marathon had been his idea, and though she was lame, she joined him without hesitation. They had managed to last for almost fifty hours before being disqualified for sleeping. Maynard was already contemplating their next move when she complained she didn't feel well. She fainted as soon as they left the dance hall. After, she had died from dehydration, and Maynard almost lost his will to live.

He found work with Hy Sugarman. Sugarman hadn't been part of a large outfit like Murder Inc., but he'd been involved with Undzer Shtik. Sugarman had made his fortune bootlegging, but his current enterprise was loansharking. When people couldn't pay the 20% vig—and rarely could they—Sugarman would ask Maynard to go collect. Maynard himself was not intimidating but when people saw Clem, they'd make whatever deal they could.

Clem had started to get worse, though. He'd have flashbacks—fine one moment, then screaming about incoming projectiles and Jerries surging over the top. The last time, Clem had almost killed the guy. To make things worse, the man had cooperated with them and given up some collateral. Clem had gotten the faraway look and started barking out commands. He had gripped the man's head with his bare hands and began to squeeze.

Maynard had touched Clem's chest, made eye contact, and was able to bring him back to reality. The man had passed out but, thankfully, had mostly recovered. Not that the guy was in a position to do anything, but still. Maynard couldn't be certain, but he assumed it had been this incident that had put him on Tuttle's radar.

The cartoon ended and a newspaper reel appeared.

The voice and photos had been about the United States' occupation of Nicaragua. Clem started making some guttural noises that Maynard recognized as warning signs of another outburst. Maynard guessed it was seeing photos of dead bodies. The crowd around them quieted and a child started to cry; it wouldn't be long before someone alerted security.

Maynard was able to steer Clem outside. Once he was in daylight, Clem returned to his old self. Maynard made a mental note to confiscate the bayonet Clem had kept as a souvenir and carried on him.

"Let's go," Maynard said.

Clem seemed disappointed he was going to miss the next showing. "A few more?" Clem said.

"How many times you seen 'em?" Maynard asked.

Clem's face soured, but he followed Maynard when he started to walk. Out in the sunlight, both of their eyes took a moment to adjust. Clem's overalls had been big on him, but now they sagged.

"We going to wear the signs today?" Clem asked.

"No."

Maynard calmly went over the plan again, even though it wasn't the first time. Maynard's stomach growled. Once they got Prince Randian, Maynard would have a steak, if any place still served them. The last time he'd had a steak was maybe '27.

Tuttle probably still had steak.

Tuttle had been hired to do contracts for Metro Goldwyn Mayer. His latest project was a film titled *Freaks* that was going to use legitimate sideshow performers. The idea developed over time once he reviewed the insurance papers for the film. The cast was unique and couldn't be replaced. If one of them was held for ransom, the studio would have no choice but to pay.

Tuttle had needed operatives to execute the plan. Clem and Maynard would pose as part of the production, go to the commissary during lunch, and take Prince Randian, one of the cast members, who had neither arms nor legs.

One of the tangents on which Tuttle had expounded was of a scene from the film he'd watched in which Prince Randian used nothing but his mouth to light a cigarette while an able-bodied man watched.

"The film's done?" Maynard had said.

"They're still editing. I was able to watch this scene ahead of time," Tuttle had said and gone back to his story.

When he was finished lighting his cigarette, Prince Randian asked the man whether the man could do anything with his eyebrows? The way Tuttle explained the caper, it would be simple; no more standing in bread lines, wearing job-seeking placards, or any of the other indignities. Tuttle had already arranged for their entrance on the lot. The following day, Clem and Maynard entered the commissary and saw their target.

Prince Randian sat at a table with a few other cast members. A woman who sat next to him, either a nurse or his wife, fed him soup. Timothy Eck, the amazing half-boy, sat with them. Eck was missing the lower half of his body. Tuttle had gone through cast photos with Maynard so there wouldn't be any confusion, but Maynard had already been familiar with Eck from Maynard's time working for Chao Kong Moon. Eck and his brother had gotten started doing a magic act and the circuit was pretty small.

The table was rounded out with a few pinheads and a woman who looked like a bird. Tuttle had mentioned the medical affliction for these final performers, but Maynard hadn't been paying attention. It didn't matter. In a few hours, he could forget all about all of it, close this unfortunate chapter of his life, and stop having nightmares about Loretta.

Maynard had walked a few steps before he realized Clem hadn't moved. He turned and saw that Clem had entered another one of his fugue states. Clem's lower lip began to tremble as he took in the sideshow performers.

"Whizbang!" Clem screamed.

The entire commissary stopped and turned their attention. Maynard rushed over to aid his friend. Maynard could only imagine that seeing the limbless actors had triggered Clem, who probably imagined he was back in the trenches on the Western Front.

"*Boche!*" Clem yelled. It was what they had called the German soldiers.

"Easy," Maynard said and touched Clem's arm.

Clem's eyes grew wide.

Maynard was able to walk a few feet with the bayonet protruding from his chest ... before he collapsed.

... IS MACHINE ... ILL ...

The Scowling Man

The Scowling Man rubbed the rest of his cocaine across his gums and when he finished, touched the handle of the nickel-plated .22 he had shoved in the waistline of his pants. He had been alternating between drinking whiskey and doing lines for the last thirty hours straight in a futile attempt to find perfect equilibrium.

It had been one of the great philosophical debates throughout history.

Though it may not have been conceived with regard to abusing narcotics—the concept of perfect balance and harmony—people had spent their lives devoted to this achievement. Confucius spoke of *The Doctrine of the Mean*; Aristotle had the "golden mean". And now, The Scowling Man sought to perfect this application for euphoria. Some would suggest this pursuit already existed in the phrase "chasing the dragon", but that metaphor had been co-opted from a more literal action in which an inhalant was constantly shifted within a container so the liquid wouldn't coalesce; this allowed for the smoke to remain manageable.

After watching *The Hitcher*, a film in which the protagonist is terrorized by a hitchhiker for no reason, The Scowling Man wondered whether it would be plausible and somehow satisfying to replicate. He'd been sitting on the N train for hours, waiting for the moment to arrive. He conjured scenes in which he produced the gun on a packed car, people trampling each other and displaying vile acts of self-preservation as he unloaded a full clip, all the while singing the lyrics to the Mission of Burma song, "That's When I Reach for My Revolver".

> *Once I had my heroes*
> *And once I had my dreams.*
> *But all of that is changed now.*
> *They've turned things inside out.*
> *The truth is not that comfortable, no!*

He touched the barrel of the weapon, gripped it like a phallus numerous times throughout the day, always while staring at someone; he realized it was strangely enjoyable. The piece was cold when he first set it in the waistband. Since then, it had warmed up; now, it felt like an extension.

He just needed a sign.

The Scowling Man caressed the handle of the weapon again, felt the kinetic energy lurking throughout the metal, the jacketed slugs in the chambers ready to run at supersonic speeds.

ANDREW DAVIE

The Troubadour

The door leading to the next car opened and a kid wearing ragged clothes, ill-fitting, and ill-equipped for the weather, strummed a beaten-up acoustic guitar. He waddled toward the middle of the car and addressed the crowd. No one paid him any attention, and soon they were inundated with an off-key rendition of "The Sound of Silence".

The kid had scabs across his knuckles like braille, fingernails yellowed around the edges, and a beard bordering on Hasidic. Playing the guitar with his eyes shut, he swayed back and forth in rhythm while passengers tried and failed to avoid imagining larvae in various stages of incubation encrusted on this soiled relic.

Once finished, he passed the hat around; no one contributed. He walked to the other end of the train. Written in magic marker on the face of the guitar, to mimic Woody Guthrie's preferred ax, was "This Machine Kills Fascists". Wear and tear, neglect, and smudging had erased some of the letters to form a slogan more befitting the current owner.

The Scowling Man

The Scowling man stared at The Troubadour and wondered if this was the moment. There was something about the kid, something he wanted to obliterate. The Scowling Man imagined himself lifting the weapon from the elastic band, cocking the hammer, the manic look of desperation on the kid's face, the sheer panic and anger at the unknown. Would he scatter like a roach or, like a cornered animal, would he reveal himself to be more than capable of defending himself?

The Scowling Man anticipated lashing out against the world by doing something wholly unforgivable.

And Mother taught us patience
The virtues of restraint
And Father taught us boundaries
Beyond which we must go
To find the secrets promised us, yeah

Then, he looked out the window across the platform, and saw the words.

At first, he wondered whether he had overdosed. Worse, maybe this train car was a level of Hell Dante never saw during his voyage. Or perhaps Satan updated the circles to keep things interesting—the circle in which one was inundated with a dissonant version of a folk staple sung by a bum soured on too much wine and pharmaceuticals.

Written on the wall above the staircase was the graffiti, "Words of the Prophets".

The Troubadour

The Troubadour heard the laughter on the near-silent train and stared at the man with the perpetual scowl. The man's right hand was shoved down the front of his pants. It figured. The Troubadour had seen everything imaginable since he'd been busking. He locked eyes with the man, but only for a moment. Just another pervert.

The train lurched forward, and inertia shifted

everyone to one hundred and ten-degree angles. The doors opened, and The Troubadour walked on to the platform.

"Tand lear of the losing oors ease."

The train pulled out toward the next station.

"That's when I reach for my revolver."

"That's when it all gets blown away!"

Maybe on the next round, The Troubadour thought he'd play some Mission of Burma.

LAND OF SOME OTHER ORDER

"Knight to g5," Henricus said.

Although the phone had cut out so it only let through every other syllable. However, Kreshnik didn't have to hear it; he already knew what his opponent was going to say. It was only a matter of time before Henricus would attempt a "Fried Liver Attack", his favorite chess opening.

Kreshnik made the move on his own board and leaned his head closer to the speakerphone so he could confirm his next move. He could have made a pithy comment about Henricus's play, but he didn't. Instead, he relayed his move and looked through the scope of his rifle.

Kreshnik was on the balcony of his tenth-floor apartment. The chess set was on the table to his left and his Zastava M48 was jerry-rigged to a tripod mount to his right. The weapon was aimed at the window of Henricus's eighth-floor apartment across the way. Through the scope, Kreshnik watched as Henricus studied the board.

Henricus checked his watch. "Can we pick this back up in a few hours?" he asked.

"Flutera stopping by?"

"Yes."

"OK. How's 1400?"

"Sounds good."

Both men hung up the phone.

It was almost noon and Akira would be visiting soon anyway. Kreshnik continued to look through the scope and watched Henricus answer his front door.

Flutera entered the apartment and hugged Henricus. Even though she had weathered hardship and gotten older, she still looked beautiful. Initially, Kreshnik had felt like a voyeur watching these moments but after a while, it no longer phased him. It had been almost a year since Kreshnik had invoked the blood feud of the tradition of Kanun and now every day was the same.

Eventually, Kreshnik went inside and brewed some tea. Akira arrived soon after, and the two of them settled on the balcony. When Akira saw the rifle, he immediately began to ask questions, and Kreshnik filled him on the basics of Kanun: only males were vulnerable, and the home was considered sanctuary.

"So, he's safe as long as he doesn't leave?" Akira had asked and twisted the end of his beard.

Akira was not his given name, but a nom de guerre he had selected when he joined The French Foreign Legion. Akira and Kreshnik had become friends when they were both in Kosovo. Kreshnik filled him in on the rules and the details of the blood feud. Henricus had wronged Kreshnik's family—a land dispute, though Kreshnik didn't go into the details. Truthfully, he had forgotten most of the details, but he had presented it as if trying to remember them was too painful.

"The second he leaves his apartment, it's fair game," Kreshnik said.

Akira paused before asking the next question, as if he were digesting the answer. How long do these feuds usually last?"

"It depends."

Kreshnik went on to suggest that sometimes things ended pretty quickly if the target was eliminated, or the wronged party compensated. Of course, he'd also heard of examples that had lasted for over a decade. He went on to explain the various laws of Kanun and how they overruled Albania's legislature. Of course, the practice had fallen off during the rise of Communism but was revived after the regime had been ousted in the early 90s.

If Henricus left the confines of his home, he could be killed. However, people could visit him and bring him supplies. They would be safe. Flutera came by twice a week. Kreshnik had not revealed that he and Henricus had grown up together, and Kreshnik had almost asked Henricus's sister, Flutera, to marry him once upon a time, he thought to himself. He also didn't mention a recent encounter when she'd tried to seduce Kreshnik and made offers, should Kreshnik leave her brother alone.

The conversation stalled as both men sipped their tea. Akira, fascinated, asked if he could look through the scope into the target's apartment. As he looked through the rangefinder, he continued to ask questions. "What if he leaves through the back?"

"I'd know. I have a motion-activated camera back there."

Akira stood up and looked at Henricus. "What about you?" he asked.

"What do you mean?"

"Do *you* ever leave?"

"Of course." Kreshnik tried to sound like the question had been ridiculous, but the truth was that, except for necessary trips, he rarely left. He even had his food delivered from the grocery store.

Akira stood up again and stretched. This time, he noticed the chessboard resting against the side of the balcony and gestured to it.

"It passes the time," Kreshnik said.

Kreshnik had forgotten whether it had been he or Henricus who had suggested playing. Both of them had boards and pieces. They could speak on the phone and keep track of each other's moves. They never kept score, so Kreshnik didn't know who had won more games and over time, it just became part of his everyday routine.

Soon, the conversation with Akira drifted to another topic, and they asked each other about some of their former comrades. Kreshnik had lost touch with most of them; Akira had been steadfast in keeping contact. Akira revealed what he knew about their inner circle. They spoke for another twenty minutes or so, until Akira said he had to leave, but they would stay in touch. They wished each other well.

When Kreshnik sat down again, it was almost 1400. He checked the rangefinder and saw Henricus was alone, sitting at the table in front of the chessboard. Kreshnik pressed the speed dial and watched as Henricus picked up the phone.

"You ready to continue?" Kreshnik inquired.

NOTHING GOOD EVER HAPPENED OUTSIDE OF A WAFFLE HOUSE AT 3 AM

The Stanley Cup went to war in 2007 ... literally. As a way to boost morale, The Cup was taken to Camp Nathan Smith in Kandahar. On the day of the attack, the people in the Humvee included Sgt. Beakman, as well as Patrick, the keeper of The Cup, responsible for its wellbeing.

Beakman and his squad had been assigned for a protection detail, even though he had been scheduled to deploy on a search and destroy mission. A congressman who'd known about Beakman's service record had demanded he and members of his team serve as the security detail while The Cup made the rounds. It wasn't that Beakman disliked hockey or wanted to rob members of his outfit of the opportunity to see it. He had grown up in a city which didn't support a hockey team, so it didn't matter to him.

He'd been a history buff, and he had been interested in the region since reading about Charlie Wilson and Gust Avrakotos's efforts to arm the Mujahideen and rid themselves of occupying Russian forces. Of course, times had changed, but his fascination with the region remained. Also, McGinty was a diehard Buffalo Sabres fan and had been asking questions incessantly since they'd gotten on the road.

"Is it true it's served soup?" McGinty asked.

He was still a kid, from someplace in upstate New York, with red hair and freckles, and he wore the highest-numbered sunblock available. The keeper of The Cup, Patrick, a middle-aged guy, wore a unit-issued helmet and protective vest, and had grayish hair that came down past his ears. When they'd boarded the Humvee, McGinty had joked about whether they should place a protective vest over The Cup. Patrick replied it was unnecessary since the case had been specially designed to withstand almost anything.

"I heard some players had their children baptized in it," McGinty said.

"Some have," Patrick replied.

He managed to stay courteous, even though Beakman knew he must have answered the same questions hundreds of times. No one spoke for a moment, and then McGinty proceeded with more queries. Beakman reminded himself if The Cup felt into Taliban hands, or worse, it would be a catastrophe.

Their escort had gained some speed and Ramirez accelerated as well. Their ETA was still good to make the checkpoint for a meet-and-greet with The Cup before it needed to circulate through the region. The road had been secured recently, but it still wasn't the sort of place you'd want to stop, like the parking lot of a fast-food joint early in the morning. Beakman figured he'd stay quiet and listen to McGinty ask questions. Of course, he was unable to do that.

"Gin, you wanna give it a rest for a minute?"

McGinty was about to reply when an IED exploded underneath the front left tire. The car flipped over backward. Thankfully, all of them had been wearing their seatbelts. However, that didn't help Ramirez, who was killed by the explosion. It took a moment for Beakman to get his bearings as his senses had been scrambled.

A high-pitched siren rang in his ears and as he craned his head to look in the rear, he saw mouths move but heard no sound. He was able to get his Reeve knife and cut through the seatbelt. The door had already opened, and he rolled out onto the road. He crawled on his hands and knees.

When sound returned, he could already hear Patrick yelling from within the cab to make sure The Cup was secure. You had to admire the guy's dedication. Beakman also heard McGinty radio for help.

Beakman opened the door. Both McGinty and Patrick were upside-down, strapped into their seats. "Sit rep!" he yelled.

Both men swiveled their heads at the same time. Neither answered. Battered, bruised, and possibly concussed, they were still acclimating, although they didn't appear to have life-threatening injuries. The case had landed near Patrick, who recognized it immediately and scrambled to maneuver it out as best he could.

Beakman was about to argue to treat the wounded first, but since The Cup was within reach, he helped slide the rest of it out. Almost as soon as he stood the case up, he heard bullets ping from it. *The Cup had saved his life.*

Later, when they'd been rescued, Beakman swore he would follow hockey for the rest of his days, maybe even become a fan of The Sabres.

PERENNIAL

The temperature in the kitchen had eclipsed rational description and moved on to religious analogy. How anyone could drink tea under these conditions was incomprehensible, but it was one of the few things John could keep down.

Vernon felt the sweat pool in the concave areas of his body. It stuck his now soaked-through clothes to his skin. He dreamed of the plunk the leader would make as it broke the water's plane when he could fish in the stream behind the house. Even now, amidst the terrible humidity, he could imagine the cool water at his knees as he stood in the riverbed, isolated from the world.

Driven by a need to satisfy his desire, he walked toward the front door but stopped and chased the thought from his head; there would be plenty of time for that later, after John had his tea. Vernon sat in the chair and dragged a handkerchief across his forehead. Instantly, the rag darkened in color and was shoved unmercifully into his pocket. His white hair itched from the humidity; he felt all his sixty years.

They were off the Carolina coast, an hour from

the next soul. At one point in time, it was a lively place. Sarah would often host events at the house. However, it had been quiet since her demise. Now, her son John haunted the top floor. Suffering from the debilitating effects of Parkinson's, he seldom left the confines of his bedroom. Sometimes, he would be in a daze and mutter half-delirious truths or old vendettas against former rivals; other times, he was lucid and precise enough to recall vividly the details of his rhino hunt.

The kettle built up to a slow roar and Vernon rose out of his chair. His back seized on him, but just for a moment. He pushed the kettle onto another burner and waited for the whistle to subside. He poured honey into a mug; the faint smell of lilac from the bag permeated the kitchen. His massive, calloused hands scooped the mug on the tray. He let the bag steep for a moment, then started the journey to the master chamber.

As a young man, Vernon had spent most of his time in and out of juvenile detention centers for petty crimes, until a grand theft auto conviction graduated him to felony status, and he enrolled in gladiator school at Angola Prison under the supervision of Associate Warden Fogarty. Throughout his tenure, Vernon felt less than human, relegated to having to do things he'd sooner forget.

His first week in, he'd made the mistake of earning the ire of Thor. It wasn't the guard's given name, but he possessed long blonde hair and at six-six, the requisite frame. The most imposing hack in the prison, Thor doled out punishments with little provocation. Instead of the department issued nightstick, he'd fashioned a shillelagh twice the size of regulations.

The warden dismissed the excessive force complaints since Thor kept order within the realm of the walls. The prisoners stayed in line when he walked the tiers, the only thing which mattered come election time. Vernon had long since forgotten the details, the circumstances which made him a marked man in Thor's eyes, but suffice to say, he still bore the scars. He would never have trouble remembering the altercation which led to Thor's death, though.

The investigation into the murder proved to be fruitless, as there had been too many suspects, but the investigators had marveled at the brutal violence and compared the attack to that of a wild animal.

Vernon stopped before the bedroom door and placed the tray on the floor. He opened the door and looked through the opening. John, now an emaciated form, lay in bed.

"I have your tea," Vernon said.

As usual, there was no response. There was virtually nothing anymore. The quiet used to trouble Vernon. Now, he barely noticed it. Vernon brought the tray over and laid it on the end table. John stared at the ceiling. His eyes were faded but retained some energy. In the past, Vernon might have tried to start a conversation. However, this time, he simply walked out of the room and began his long trip down the stairs.

A BUREAUCRATIC DESIRE FOR REVENGE

It was during the prison rodeo that Vernon got his revenge. It had taken him almost a year of planning and waiting. Every time Thor walked his tier and banged his feared cudgel against the bars of the cells, it felt like they were being dragged across Vernon's ribcage. Now, as he stood in the corner of the horse's paddock, he gripped the fiberglass shiv so hard, for a moment, he thought he might crack it.

He had finished grooming Cinnamon, whose head was buried in a pail of oats. The smell of hay was thick. It was silent except for the occasional neigh from a horse in a nearby stall. Thor would arrive soon. He was going to lead Cinnamon to the arena, then grab a quick smoke; at least, that's what Vernon's recon had told him. It had cost him his desserts for the next six months to get that information, but it would be worth it.

Vernon could practically hear his heart beating through his chest. He flinched every time a noise sounded from outside the stall. Cinnamon continued to chew loudly, without ever taking her head out of the bucket. Eventually, footfalls echoed on the landing and stopped outside Cinnamon's stall.

The door slid back, and Thor stepped inside. As Thor turned to shut the door, Vernon was already on him. Vernon hadn't studied any anatomy textbooks, so he didn't know which was the most lethal place to strike. He figured to try and cover the maximum area possible.

Thor's back was to him when he delivered his barrage. Thor had bellowed with surprise after the first strike. He probably would have screamed in pain after the next few, but the wind had been knocked out of him.

The coroner's report would later list the cause of death to be a combination of shock, organ failure, and severe blood loss. When Thor had stopped convulsing, Vernon rolled him onto his back. Vernon worked on him for another few seconds. When he finished, the horse had finally raised her head. She still chewed her oats, but now she stared at Vernon. Soon, however, she went back to her food.

Vernon broke the weapon into smaller pieces and threw them down a drain in the corner of the stall. Then he hosed down the area. He figured he'd have another few minutes or so before anyone came to look for Thor.

Vernon slid back the partition and stepped onto the landing. It was clear. He made his way back to the stands and blended in with the audience. Ten minutes later, when Thor's body had been discovered, the alarm sounded, and the prisoners were rounded up and bused back to the penitentiary.

Over the next few days, the administration raised hell. Ultimatums and threats were issued. The rodeo would be canceled for the next few years, and more sanctions were placed on the prison population. While it may have curried favor with the inmates, Vernon never let anyone know he was responsible. Over the years, various convicts would take credit; some of their claims were debunked, others weren't.

In the end, Vernon was content to do his time peacefully now that Thor was out of the picture.

"Vernon." John's voice was dry and cracked.

"Yes?"

Vernon had just set the tray with the tea on the end table. He had already turned to leave and take a few steps when John spoke. John's eyes were unfocused, and he launched into a recollection of when he had hunted a rhinoceros in Namibia.

It had been something he had wanted to do his entire life. It caused quite a stir when part of the funding came from a non-profit group that granted "wishes" to people dealing with illnesses. John had always claimed the animal had been in a full charge and stopped before he could gore John, his guide, or any of the other hunters in their group. He went on to suggest how it was as if the animal had dared them to act.

John had steadied his nerves and aimed his weapon. Both continued to stare at each other until John's compatriots opened fire at point-blank range. The animal remained upright for a few more seconds, took some steps forward, swayed, and fell to the ground. The other members of the group continued to fire to ensure the beast had been killed. Of course, whether it had happened this way remained to be seen.

Vernon had been skeptical the animal would have stopped mid-charge, but he never said anything. He probably could have tracked down someone from the group to verify John's version of the events, but it didn't matter enough to him to do so. The trip had seemed to reinvigorate John, and he would often stare at the photo that had been taken of him and his trophy.

Vernon had heard the story so many times, he

could probably recite it verbatim. The first time he'd heard it, he had just started to work as a caretaker for the family. John had been diagnosed with Parkinson's, and though the symptoms hadn't progressed to the point where he needed full-time care, John's mother Sarah could use the help, especially since her husband had passed a few years previously.

Even though Vernon had served time, the family was willing to overlook it. He was one of the few applicants they had seen who had had medical experience. Of course, he had only worked in the prison infirmary as an orderly, but most healthcare workers had balked at the prospective salary. Vernon had agreed to less than what they had offered and seemed genuinely enthusiastic about the chance to help John.

When he started to work for the family, he had rented a room nearby. In the beginning, he helped around the house. He changed lightbulbs when it was needed, did the grocery shopping, and the laundry. Sarah worked full time providing bookkeeping for a few companies in town. At the end of the day, she and Vernon would play canasta as a way for her to decompress.

She had learned how to play the game after she had spent some time doing missionary work in South America and developed an affinity for it. After she had returned home, it didn't take long before she introduced the game to her friends. Often, she would lead a Bible study group and after a break, they would split into teams for a few games of canasta. At the end of each day, though, Sarah and Vernon would enjoy each other's company. Their relationship was always one of mutual support and never became romantic. Though it certainly could have gone that way, both regarded the other as a necessary component in the other's life to provide a sense of solace and nothing more.

A few years later, after Sarah died and John's condition deteriorated, Vernon moved into Sarah's old room. He kept it relatively empty. Except for some fishing gear, and a few books, it was spartan. His list of duties grew exponentially until John needed around-the-clock care. He switched from canasta to solitaire.

"Is there anything I can do, Mr. Tarden?" Vernon asked.

John stopped talking and his eyes came back into focus. It was as if he seemed to notice Vernon for the first time that afternoon. Very slowly, he reached to the side of his bed and opened the drawer of the end table. His movements were deliberate, and he ground his teeth as he put forth concerted effort. His hand came back with a Smith & Wesson .38 service revolver. It had belonged to John's grandfather, who had been a sheriff. John brought back the hammer and pointed the weapon at Vernon. The two men stared at each other for a moment before John broke the silence again.

"I know," he said.

John had emerged from his haze and, for the first time in a while, seemed cognizant. He was in his mid-forties now but appeared to be much older due to the effects of his condition. John turned his head slightly, so he could gaze at the bottom shelf on the left side of the room where the shillelagh had been displayed. It was one of the various possessions which had been issued to the family after the funeral and the execution of the will. Next to the weapon were two framed photos: one of John with the rhino and the other a newspaper article that detailed the demise of James Tarden while in the line of duty.

Vernon stared at the shillelagh for a long time before he addressed John.

"There's something else you should know," Vernon said. "There are no bullets in that gun." Vernon's voice strained as if it had taken a Herculean effort to speak. Tears had formed, though he wasn't aware of them. Absentmindedly, he wiped them from his face.

John's eyes were shrewd. Another moment passed and the gun didn't waver.

Vernon sighed audibly and slowly reached into his pocket. He produced a gravity knife and opened it. The blade caught some of the light and it danced on the wall above John's head. Vernon felt a rush of emotions long thought to be dormant.

The following day, Vernon cast his line in the water. The leader plopped into the darkness and he pulled the line taught. He waited a moment and picked up a can of beer from the water with his feet. He popped the top and took a long pull.

Very little would change in terms of his day-to-day life; there were still chores to be done around the house. He would just have more free time. The solitude might be difficult, but he had endured worse, so he knew he was ready for the challenge. It had been months since anyone had inquired about Sarah and, aside from insurance claims, he doubted anyone would check on John. Besides, it wouldn't be difficult to settle John's estate. It would take time, but he had plenty of that now. He doubted anyone would investigate.

Vernon looked over his shoulder at the recently filled hole. He had eulogized the body, even though he was the only person present. Though he felt conflicted, John would not be buried near his parents, Vernon knew he would reconcile the feeling over time. He killed his beer, reached into the water, and produced another one. He depressed the tab, and foam spilled over the lip of the can. He dragged his handkerchief over his brow. It was going to be a hot afternoon indeed.

PRIMER

The disease had ravaged her body. She bore little resemblance to the woman she once was, but he still loved her. He'd long since forgotten what day it was. Gray stubble covered his cheeks and made him look older than his forty-five years. The smell of the stale broth on the nightstand and the odor of her soiled bedspread no longer caused him to recoil. He picked up a partially melted ice cube and dragged it across her cracked lips, watched the light refracting on the droplet's surface and glisten against her skin.

It wouldn't be long now.

He gripped her hand within his own. He could feel the pronounced tendons underneath her skin. Her fingers curled slightly, exerted pressure, and her eyes flashed. For a moment, the color returned to her face, and he leaned forward. Her throat constricted. He placed his ear near her mouth and felt the warm foulness exhale along with her words.

"I love you, Arthur."

She died, and he wept.

He looked at her sunken form. Bottles of medication covered the nightstand. The writing was foreign to him. He fled the bedroom. The living room was in perfect order, which was somehow an affront to the chaos in his life. He stepped over to his desk, a big rolltop monstrosity, opened the drawers, and rummaged around. He finally found it underneath his checkbook and shoved it into his front pocket.

The front door opened. He began walking in earnest, following the path which led from their cottage to the road. He heard the sound of the machine before he saw it on the horizon. The transport carried soldiers from the Belgian Explosive Ordinance Division.

The man stood to the side of the road and watched the truck pass by. Six of them, decked out in Demon Suits, sat on the truck bed. Most paid him no attention, content to discuss the score of last night's FC Brussels game or enjoy a quick smoke before the task at hand. The truck disappeared down the road. It was the Iron Harvest. Farmers would plow their fields and the disposal unit would collect any unexploded ordnance from the first war.

He continued walking, veered left, and thought about the soldiers from that generation on the front who operated the mortars and shelled the countryside. He imagined the oxidation, the corrosion, and the iron deposits poisoning the soil and the water supply. He imagined his wife drinking that water. He thought of melanoma, carcinoma, cell replication, nature's retribution against such a gross violation by mankind.

He crossed the road and approached the first house. He noted the contours of the thatched roof and the color of the wood which had been used to fabricate the front door. He heard nothing but the sound of the chimes rattling against each other from the wind.

He knocked on the door and felt his heartbeat rise in his chest. Sweat dripped from his palms. He reached into his pocket. The door opened to reveal a slender-looking man. All the man's features worked in harmony with his character: green eyes, blonde hair, deep tan. The slender man would have said hello and welcomed his guest inside.

The gun spoke instead.

The report was louder than he expected, and his ears rang. His hand jumped as he continued to squeeze the trigger, but three bullets hit center mass. The slender man fell backward, his shirt turning from white to crimson. Garbled words escaped from the man's mouth, and he lay sprawled on the floor. He let the gun drop to the ground and watched Arthur's slender body convulse in awkward gestures, then cease altogether.

SOMETIMES THEY WOULDN'T
GO AWAY

Rainbow Row was the name given to a set of houses on East Bay Street in downtown Charleston, South Carolina. It was rumored the houses had been painted different colors because they used to be storefronts, and illiterate people could differentiate between the stores based on the colors. Others had said it had to do with temperature control; since it was so hot, the colors would act as a natural coolant. Another rumor was the houses were painted in these loud colors so intoxicated sailors, who had secured lodging, could make their way back to their bunks at night by remembering the colors.

Eric preferred to believe the last one.

He would have been one of those sailors had he been born in a different time. More than likely, he would have been a pirate. In the 1700s, Charleston had been home to several pirates. At one point, it was even the stomping ground of Blackbeard. It wouldn't have turned out well for Eric, though.

In 1718, nearly 50 pirates had been hanged. A carriage full of tourists trotted by and broke him from his daydream. The Clydesdales' hooves sounded on the cobblestones. Eric couldn't see either the horses or the houses from his vantage point on the boat, but he could hear the echo of their footfalls. He wondered which historical fact the driver was reciting.

The wind picked up. Some of Mr. McClaren's white hair that had been caught in the zipper fluttered as it got caught in the breeze, and Eric had to laugh. When he was alive, McClaren had been so concerned with his appearance, he kept a comb in his front pocket.

McClaren's body, still in the duffle bag, had been wedged under the gunwale on the bow of the boat. It had taken Eric months of planning to finally put everything in motion. Getting the job had been easy enough since so few candidates had lasted for more than a day. Eric was different, though. He had the endurance. However, he'd had to ingratiate himself to McClaren, which had been a challenge since the man had been a misanthrope. Eric had invested hours in listening to McClaren recount the same stories of how he'd amassed his fortune, bested competitors; most of the stories were similar variations of the first.

Since it had gotten oppressively humid, McClaren would end the day with a cocktail. His daughter wouldn't approve, but as McClaren often said, "I'm the one who signs your checks."

So, at five o'clock, Eric would fix McClaren a mint julep. The old man had been very particular about the ratio of simple syrup to rum. A mistake with his beverage was one thing McClaren wouldn't tolerate.

McClaren didn't taste the antifreeze Eric had mixed in when making the latest drink.

Eric had doubled the lethal amount; McClaren had assumed Eric had added too much syrup and let him have it. Later that same evening, McClaren had begun to feel some of the symptoms but assumed they had been caused by indigestion. In the morning, he awoke delirious and nauseated, with difficulty breathing. He died soon thereafter.

Eric wouldn't be able to clearly articulate his motives; he hadn't been abused as a child. He didn't suffer from PTSD. It was nothing like that. He just couldn't grind it out anymore. Eric needed a change. He had been tempted to transfer some of McClaren's holdings but didn't want to arouse the curiosity of a portfolio manager.

Instead, Eric ransacked the home for enough valuables that would put him on easy street for a long time. He had also made all the arrangements and left signs to indicate McClaren would be going to take the boat to visit friends down the coast in Florida for a few weeks.

His daughter would be happy he'd taken the trip. Whether anyone eventually figured it out, Eric would have a few weeks head start, and that was all he needed. Early the morning of McClaren's demise, Eric let himself into the apartment, cleaned everything, and stowed McClaren's body in a duffel bag. There were only three apartments on the floor. Currently, both places were empty as the neighbors only lived there part-time.

The elevator went directly to the underground parking garage. When he got down there, Eric loaded the duffle into the trunk of his Datsun. He'd leave it in a parking lot near the marina and pay for a few weeks. It had taken some maneuvering to get McClaren in the trunk since the body had begun to undergo the effects of rigor mortis but eventually Eric was able to make it fit.

A quick ride to the ocean and before long Eric was out on the water. He had stowed the duffle under the gunwale. They were going to head to open water. Eric would find a spot far enough out, weigh down the body, sink it, and head off to The Bahamas; from there, who knew? Eric took one last look at Charleston as the boat continued to drift. He turned the key in the ignition and piloted the boat further out into the ocean.

The saltwater sprayed his face as he traveled. Along the way, he allowed himself to think of what life would be like now, the fantasies of what awaited. He cut the power and walked to the body. He spent the next few minutes wrapping a chain around the duffle bag so it wouldn't come undone in the water. The other end of the chain was affixed to an anchor. He lifted the body and placed it against the railing. He would toss the anchor into the water and, once taut, it would pull the duffle overboard.

Eric would set sail to paradise. He picked up the anchor. Suddenly, he found himself off balance; he was going into the water. He'd managed to drop the anchor onto the bow of the boat before he'd fallen. As he gained his composure and swam toward the surface, he realized it must have been a combination of things that caused him to sway: a rush of blood, the waves, possible dehydration.

"Well done," a voice said when Eric broke the plane.

Eric scanned the deck, though he knew he was the only one there. The voice sounded like McClaren's.

"Now what?" the voice asked.

Eric swam over to the railing and tried to hoist himself up, but it was too difficult. He hadn't begun to panic, but he knew that would set in soon if he wasn't able to figure this out.

"Good idea," the voice said.

"Shut up," Eric snapped.

He closed his eyes, took a few deep breaths, and tried to calm himself. Once panic began to set in, he would have a difficult time ridding himself of it. Nothing but more ocean in every direction. Thankfully, it was a calm and sunny day. One of two things could happen—like a boat would come by and rescue him.

"How would you explain this?" the voice asked.

He couldn't bring himself to think about the second thing, at least not yet.

"What about a shark?" the voice questioned.

"Only in the movies," Eric said, then shook his head and questioned whether he had begun to go insane.

"Alright, what's the second option?"

Eric wouldn't entertain the thought.

"You better conserve your energy," the Voice began. "Who knows how long you'll have to stay afloat."

Eric lay on his back and stared at the sky. There wasn't a single cloud.

"Keep an eye out for 'gators, too," the Voice advised.

Alligators were indigenous to the area and though it was extremely rare, they had been seen swimming in the ocean before.

"Not likely," Eric said.

"Not likely, eh? What were the odds you'd fall into the drink?" The voice had said this in the same manner as McClaren's tone, which would always get under Eric's skin.

"Shut up!" Eric yelled.

The voice was silent for a moment. "Turn around."

Eric did a quick 180 in the water and saw a sailboat tacking toward them.

"Good luck explaining everything," the Voice said.

THE BODYSNATCHER

It was an all-consuming fire that had sprung up from nothing, calm one moment and pandemonium the next. Gordon imagined Hell must have started the same way. The train compartment was now fully engulfed in flames. Smoke billowed from the roof into one giant cloud, which blocked out the sun and brought on premature darkness. The sight of dead bodies caused some of the hostages to retch. Some of them had to stop walking to steady themselves.

The thieves had already been aboard the train, waited until it was half an hour out of the city, shot the brakeman, and had begun to loot the passengers before the train had screeched to a halt. The thieves had been upset by the revelation more of the passengers had been carrying travelers' checks than they had anticipated. So, they took what valuables they could and figured they would increase the numbers for ransom.

Gordon had been on tour with King Copen, a jazz musician, and his band. Gordon had worked for the man since the mid-1920s. The man would travel by car and meet them at the venue, but Gordon and the rest of the band would take the train along with the instruments and gear. Gordon worked as a technician, but mostly his job included escorting Copen to an opium den and taking care of him after he'd gotten righteous. The man was a hophead, but he was also a talented musician.

In most of the big cities they toured, Copen would have a regular place. Gordon didn't have to protect the man as much as watch over him. For example, if there was a raid, Gordon would make sure to grease the lead officer. If there were newspapermen there, Gordon would escort Copen out the back. These occurrences were rare, though they weren't impossible.

The thieves approached the band and made their demands of valuables. The band and technicians offered whatever they had.

One of the thieves noticed the cases of instruments. "What're these?"

"That's Bertha," "Lip" McCutcheon said and pointed to his horn.

"What?" The tone of the question was more confusion than anger.

"My horn, man," McCutcheon replied. There was anger in his tone.

Gordon was about to suggest Lip let it go. The thief grabbed the case and yanked it onto the floor. Lip was out of his seat and already cursing the thief for disrespecting his horn. The thief shot Lip before Lip could finish issuing his threat.

When the sound returned, no one argued when they were ordered off the train and told to leave their belongings behind. They had gotten within one hundred feet of the train when there was an explosion. Everyone turned to look. The coal car was ignited.

"Keep movin'," one of the thieves ordered.

He was a greasy looking kid, no more than twenty, with a tangle of strawberry blonde hair that peaked from underneath his cap. They had all worn handkerchiefs over their mouths and noses, but most of them had lowered them. The kid tore off a plug of tobacco and chewed. The juice escaped through his bottom teeth and ran down his chin.

Everyone started walking again.

Gordon glanced at the man behind them with the drum gun. He was barrel-chested but had a lean countenance, and he knew his way around the weapon. His handiwork lay sprawled behind them, riddled with bullet holes. One of the hostages, not a member of the band but someone who'd tried to hide in the restroom of their train car, piped up. He wore a tailored suit and had a handlebar mustache. "If you gentlemen let me go--."

"Shut yer trap," the kid hissed and hit the man with the butt of his firearm. The weapon met the skull, which made a sound similar to a fresh watermelon being split. The man fell and, in doing so, took down the person who'd been walking next to him. The hostages stopped.

"Well, help him up," the kid said to no one in particular.

Another man, a mousy looking fellow with knock knees, helped the wounded man to his feet. The kid waved them on again. They continued for another half an hour or so, until they reached the ridgeline of a forest. The man with the drum gun produced a corncob pipe. He flicked the match head with his thumb and lit the bowl.

"Uh, sir," the mousy prisoner piped up. He was a docile fellow, and Gordon could tell it took all his constitution to speak. He had also soiled himself.

"This man needs help."

The prisoner with the head injury had begun frothing at the mouth like a rabid dog. The wound had turned sour. He was semi-conscious and started to convulse. The kid raised his weapon and fired; it was practically point-blank, and the impact sent the man airborne.

"He don't need help no more," the kid said and cackled.

The forest was a treacherous crossing of overgrown thickets and brambles. Sounds of insects resonated, and the stink of a swamp permeated the air. It was slow going, with the men sinking up to their knees in the muck. An audible pop emanated every time they retracted their feet from the sediment. Eventually, the ground hardened and the men found their rhythm again.

In the distance, Gordon heard the faint vibration of conversation. About fifty feet away, the trees had been felled to create an opening big enough to set up camp for about twenty men. A cast-iron pot hung from a makeshift spit over a flame. Gordon smelled the stewed meat, and his stomach growled. In the distance, Gordon saw the man with the drum gun talking to someone whom Gordon could only imagine was their leader.

The leader nodded as the drum gun man spoke and rubbed the tip of his van dyke. After they had finished their conversation, the leader walked over to address the hostages.

"Gentlemen, my name is Clyde Beaumont," he said. "I promised my men something worthwhile today, and y'all have the chance to not make me out a liar." He folded his arms across his chest.

He exuded an immortality Gordon had only seen a few times in his travels: people who'd stared death in the face and dodged the scythe. His men would suffer and ultimately succumb to bullet wounds or worse, but Clyde Beaumont would live.

The kid had wormed his way to the front, directly to the left of Beaumont, and he rubbed his hands together with delight.

"Now we gonna have some fun," he said and bit his plug of tobacco. The drum gun man stood off in the distance, the cherry ember of his pipe glowing with every inhalation.

Beaumont was joined by an enormous man who looked like a mountain come to life. He had muttonchop sideburns and wore army-issue pants with suspenders and no shirt. His forearms were a latticework of veins and sinew.

"Gentlemen, this is Willis Dauterive. He went thirty-eight rounds with Seamus O'Connell and would have beaten that bastard if the referee hadn't blundered it."

Dauterive spat on the ground as if to echo the sentiment. The hostages collectively groaned. Mousy relieved himself again.

"You will all be given the chance to challenge Mr. Dauterive. If you can remain standing after three rounds, well, you are then free to go."

Beaumont's men laughed. One of the hostages,

who had realized their fates had been sealed, attempted to flee.

"No," Mousy repeated again and tore off toward the tree line. He got about ten feet from the group when a pistol shot rang out.

Beaumont lowered the weapon and placed it back in his waistline. "It ain't up for debate," he said.

The first man was selected from the hostages. He was a young fellow who had maintained his composure throughout, even with a firearm in his face. He walked to meet Dauterive and rolled up the sleeves to his shirt. Both men lifted their hands, open-palmed, to show they weren't holding anything, and commenced.

Dauterive toyed with the man at first. He presented his chin while he kept his hands lowered. The man threw a reckless punch and Dauterive kicked him in the seat of his pants. Two of the crew on the edge of the circle, who had been attempting to get odds on the match, stopped their attempts.

The drum gun man kept time and called out, "One minute left in the round."

Dauterive threw a jab, which stunned the man, then a right cross, which separated the man from his senses. The man lay still with arms akimbo. Blood flowed freely from his now broken nose. Beaumont walked over to the man and put a bullet in his chest. They dragged the body away and flung it on a developing pile, along with Mousy.

"Who's next?" Beaumont asked and kept his pistol drawn in case anyone thought to run.

"Him," the kid said and pointed toward Gordon.

"Alright, git up there."

Gordon unbuttoned his shirt and threw it to the

ground. He was a foot shorter than Dauterive, and he gave up at least thirty pounds. Dauterive stank of body odor and seemed primordial. They put their fists up and drum gun man called out to begin.

They circled each other. Gordon threw a jab, which Dauterive countered with an overhand right that snapped Gordon's head back. Gordon saw stars for a moment but shook it off. The next few seconds stretched in his imagination and suddenly Gordon was back in Leavenworth on Thanksgiving, watching the former heavyweight champion of the world box.

It had been eight years ago. The fights were scheduled to start right after the prisoners were issued Thanksgiving dinner. However, a few thousand people showed up early, including reporters and celebrities. The spectacle would take place in an outside boxing ring, and though Jack Johnson was past his prime, he was still a force.

Gordon and his cell block had been escorted outside by armed guards and sat in a special section for prisoners. All around them flashbulbs popped off as Johnson made his way to the ring. Reporters frantically jockeyed for better positions among a sea of soldiers and notables. The prisoners had been told ahead of time there would also be snipers positioned around the yard. None of them had any thoughts on their minds other than watching the former champion. While Gordon had been a casual fan before that moment, he swore he would dedicate himself to boxing.

Most of the following blows thudded against his forearms. Dauterive hit like a mule. Gordon attempted to keep on the balls of his feet. He countered with a left-right combination, which Dauterive parried and put Gordon down with a left jab, followed by a right uppercut. Gordon arose on unsure footing but adjusted quickly. He shook the cobwebs loose. He had Dauterive's timing now.

Gordon sought out anyone who would help him. It didn't take long to find a few candidates, but only one who was willing to teach him. That would be fine. Mordecai had worked in Solly Smith's camp after he had won and lost the featherweight championship. Gordon soaked up everything like a sponge.

Dauterive and Gordon exchanged some glancing blows and circled each other. Many of Beaumont's men, who'd offered bets, were now readjusting the odds. The drum gun man called time and the two combatants stopped moving and put their hands down. Dauterive called for a drink, and one of the men brought him a canteen. He took a gulp, swished the water in his mouth, and spat it out. Negotiations continued on the outskirts of the circle as more of the crew began to take bets. No one brought Gordon any water. Once again, the drum gun man called the time, and both participants continued.

Mordecai desperately needed spectacles, but it was going to take a while to go through the proper channels. It didn't make a difference, except when he wielded the end of a pipe and used it when training Gordon.

This particular exercise had Gordon working on his head movement. Every so often, Mordecai would lash out with the pipe end and Gordon would need to dodge and counter. Due to his advanced age, and curmudgeon attitude, Gordon made certain never to make contact with Mordecai, though he came close a few times. Mordecai, however, was not nearly as careful when swinging the pipe. He had already hit Gordon twice, the second of which had opened a gash near Gordon's hairline. The bleeding had stopped, but Gordon was worried he would have to explain the laceration to the duty officer. They still had another ten minutes of yard time. Both of them had found a place to work in a blind spot from the south guard tower. Jimmy Hooks, another of Mordecai's protege's, kept watch at the corner.

Time was called again, and both Gordon and Dauterive rested. Dauterive was a skilled pugilist, but Gordon could tell he was used to winning most of his fights through intimidation and ending things within the first round. By now, he had begun to breathe heavily. The same man from earlier again brought Dauterive the canteen. This time he drank down the water. The drum gun man signaled it was time to begin again, and Gordon and Dauterive walked back to the center.

"This is the final round," Beaumont said.

Upon his release, Gordon found work as a strikebreaker, but he didn't have the fury required—not to mention that within a year or two, saboteurs and spies had become more fashionable. By luck soon after that, he was able to find work for Copen. He rarely needed to get physical anymore, though the training was always there.

Gordon waited for his moment and when Dauterive threw a left hook, Gordon landed his own first. Dauterive fell to the ground and the onlookers were immediately silent. Two of the men attended to Dauterive, who was still unconscious.

"Well, I'll be damned," said Beaumont, who looked Gordon over like he'd discovered gold amongst dredged mud. "I guess you're free to go."

Gordon picked up his shirt.

"Wait, you can't," the kid said.

"You heard me say it: anyone goes three with Dauterive can walk." Beaumont's tone suggested the matter wasn't up for discussion.

The kid stared at Gordon with open hostility.

"But Uncle Clyde!" the kid whined. He hesitated for a moment, looked like he was going to reach for his firearm, but thought better of it. His face turned crimson; he let rip a series of expletives and walked away.

Gordon finished buttoning his shirt and walked

toward the edge of the woods. If he made good time, he might be able to make it back to the train tracks by sundown.

THE GOLEM

Four days before he was scheduled to die, Bill Anderson had agreed to be part of the upcoming clinical trials and had signed over the rights of his body to the Schole Corporation. Anderson disappeared the day before his execution. His vanishing encouraged the Schole Corporation to shred and redact the majority of the documents in their biomedical division out of fear of congressional oversight.

Lincoln "Linc" Schole, the grandson of the founder, eighty-three years old, had been bedridden for almost a year with aggressive kidney failure and required dialysis to clean his blood. A live-in staff of six kept the mansion spotless and spent most of their time playing poker in the servants' quarters.

Also in Linc's employ was a four-star Michelin chef and a nurse who remained by his bed twenty hours a day. Armand K, the current CEO, had only been to the compound once, on the day he was hired. He'd been flown by private helicopter over a tennis court and manicured hedged lawn and deposited in the backyard near a fleet of cars that contained a Bentley, a 1958 red and white Corvette, and a model he'd never seen before (a prototype that wouldn't be released to the public for another two years).

That day, he and Linc enjoyed a bottle of Château Lafite Rothschild 1982 while negotiating the terms of K's contract. Linc had been vibrant and alive back then, a ruggedly handsome man, a dead ringer for John Huston, down to the gravelly voice. It pained K to see Linc now, watch the man contort with every movement, his voice barely able to escape his lips.

Linc had authorized K to handle the Anderson situation by any means necessary. It was the last executive decision he would make as he died of renal failure the following week. His son, George Schole, would inherit the company but remain a figurehead, content to spend six months of the year in Florence, Italy, studying sculpture, and the other six on a private island near St. Thomas.

That first night, K assembled his team—directors of the various arms of the corporation—and had them begin the containment of what was now being referred to as "Andersonville", alluding to the infamous Confederate prisoner of war camp. The sun was rising the following day when K received a call from Willa Fye, his second in command, who'd been working with prison officials to keep the disappearance under wraps.

"What have you got?" K requested.

"The trail is cold. We're going to need to bring in the locals before it dries out entirely."

"I'll take care of it," K said. He hung up the phone.

They couldn't afford to bring in the locals without the thing leaking. He was going to have to make the call. K rummaged through the papers in his desk drawer before he found a worn business card for an upholsterer in Detroit. The card had been bestowed on him by Linc the day he'd signed his contract.

"Use this only when your back is to the wall," Linc had said cryptically.

K had only used the card once before and immediately understood the warning. The guy was the best, but the collateral damage warranted discretionary use of his services.

Banadanavitch had been putting the finishing touches on a newly upholstered couch when the phone rang. He picked up on the second ring. When K began to talk, Banadanavitch flipped a switch near the base of the phone to scramble the signal and encode the conversation. K filled him in on the details, highlighting the urgency more than once, then hung up. Banadanavitch attached the bill of lading to the sofa cushion for his apprentice to deliver later and walked out the front door.

K began to feel the anxiety gnaw at the base of his head and filter through his bloodstream until his whole body radiated as if he'd handled a dangerous isotope and became radioactive. He wondered if he'd risked too much contacting Banadanavitch. K poured himself three fingers of Scotch. He checked the time. It had been almost twenty-four hours since Anderson's escape. The phone rang: Fye.

"We found Anderson. He's dead."

K shattered the glass in his hand.

"He never even escaped from the prison," Fye continued. Anderson had been killed during an altercation with a guard. The guard wrapped up the body, dumped it in a trash bin, doctored some paperwork, and took off. They discovered Anderson's remains in a landfill a few counties over.

"Jesus," K said.

He suggested Fye return, cleaned the broken glass from his desk, and summoned his detail. All five were ex-military. Ron Joseph, K's head of security, had been with the Air Force Special Force Division for fifteen years. After his honorable discharge, he found work as a mercenary with a handpicked crew of capable but morally flexible soldiers. K briefed Joseph of the particulars regarding Banadanavitch, told him speed was of the essence, and sent him on his way.

"You can't un-ring that bell," he remembered Linc saying after he had given him Banadanavitch's business card. When they had left him, K picked up a photo from his desk: his wife and their three kids. K hadn't been home for almost two straight days.

Joseph sat in his car outside the Chevron station and took another sip from his water. He was across the highway, directly from the Western Union. K had made arrangements to wire Banadanavitch some walking-around money about a half an hour ago.

"He just went in," Joseph's earbud crackled.

"Okay."

Joseph would have preferred a long-range approach: just take Banadanavitch entirely out of the picture, but K wanted him alive. The man had secrets. No matter. Joseph and his team would accomplish the mission. Of course, he'd heard rumors about Banadanavitch, but he'd also heard rumors about Sierra Leone and Nicaragua. He would add Banadanavitch's name to his resume, and he reminded himself to put in for a bonus when this was all said and done.

Joseph finished his water and stuck the car in drive. The tension rose as it always did, a constricted feeling, but also one which heightened his senses. The pine wafted off the car air freshener; in the passenger seat, an X26 taser, Glock 9mm, and zip ties. A pregnant woman exited the Western Union. Joseph drummed his fingers on the steering wheel in time with his breathing.

A minute later, Banadanavitch walked outside. He had a beard, gray at the chin, and suffered from male pattern baldness.

Banadanavitch stopped at a Motel 6 just down the road from the Western Union. He paid cash for a room around the back, on the ground floor. The room smelled of mildew and looked like it hadn't been cleaned since the previous occupant's stay, but Banadanavitch didn't care about such things. He'd spent nights in far worse places and circumstances. He placed his piece and suppressor in the top drawer of the end table next to the Bible, sat on the bed, and turned on the television. The piece hadn't been too hard to acquire, the suppressor only slightly more so.

A BUREAUCRATIC DESIRE FOR REVENGE

After watching the predatory habits of the American Alligator, he shut his eyes and meditated for twenty minutes. He unscrewed the cap to the phone's receiver, placed his scrambler inside, dialed the numbers, and waited. The voicemail recording played for dry cleaners and ended by reiterating the hours of operation. In reality, it was a front for Agency Operations, and though his credentials were no longer good, he still had enough juice to call in a few favors.

K walked the perimeter on the roof of the building. Sometimes, when his office seemed too confined, he'd come up here. He stood near the edge. It was the fifth such revolution he'd done in the last forty minutes. The air woke him up, and the chills from the wind kept him focused. He'd always enjoyed heights, something most people could never understand. The fire department was called once when a neighbor spotted him during his grad school years on the ledge of his apartment and suspected he was going to jump. He became somewhat of a campus celebrity for a little while.

He was relaxed and stared out over the edge. The serenity acted as a counterbalance to the turbulence in his mind. Even if a probe was done into the Schole Corporation, no one would find anything incriminating. Banadanavitch would be handled soon. K turned around from the ledge, walked over to the helicopter, and touched the rotor blade. Maybe once this whole ordeal was finished, he'd take it somewhere, like a private suite in Vegas with some of the board members, or he'd take the family to a private beach somewhere in the Caribbean. His thoughts were dashed by the ringing of his cell phone. Fye again.

"Joseph and his crew are all dead; it was a massacre. The news is already ..."

The sound cut out; it was like K had entered a vacuum.

You couldn't un-ring *that* bell.

THE TREEHOUSE

"I should have been here for the funeral," Jasper said. It came out like a whisper, like he was in confessional looking for absolution, but the sound echoed throughout the clearing, nonetheless.

Jasper stopped, shut his eyes, and took a deep breath. They were almost to "Ichabog". He could wait until they were settled before broaching the subject again.

"Ichabog" was the name Ray finally settled on for the deer stand. He had originally wanted to call it "The Suck", Marine slang for bad conditions since the place got flooded frequently but went with something a little different in the end.

Jasper continued until he emerged from the path and into the clearing.

He enjoyed hunting, but he wouldn't have labeled himself a hunter, not like Ray. If they didn't get something by the end of the day, it would bother Ray. Jasper was just happy to crack a few beers and call it a win regardless.

Jasper took in the surroundings. The water had risen a few inches, but the giant willow tree was still there a few feet from the water's edge. Something behind the tree glinted in the sunlight. Unsure of what it was, Jasper took a couple steps forward. It was a shovel buried in a fresh mound of dirt next to a hold. The thoughts didn't process and confusion spread over Jasper's face.

"Ray?" Jasper asked and turned around.

Ray stood in the clearing, twenty feet away with his rifle aimed directly at Jasper.

Ray saw the bewildered look on Jasper's face. Jasper still hadn't gotten it. Ray wanted to put the rest of his plan into action, but somehow seeing the confusion on Jasper's face prevented him from doing so. He needed Jasper to understand. So, Ray would wait to pull the trigger until Jasper's eyes widened and his mouth contorted, as it finally dawned on him.

Everything had been planned meticulously—digging the hole, showing Jasper all the things in his past, leaving out the hospital bills, and making sure Jennifer's photo had been in plain view. Ray knew that if he put any more pressure on the trigger, the firing pin would ignite, and the bullet would leave the muzzle. It would hit Jasper in the stomach. The projectile might not kill him, but it would send him to the ground in a flood of pain.

Jasper still looked puzzled, but now rage had threatened to take overtake Ray. The muscles in Ray's finger tightened by a fraction, almost at the breaking point. That was when it finally happened. Jasper's face changed, but he was no longer looking at Ray. He stared over Ray's shoulder toward the water. Jasper's face had gone white. Ray heard water splash behind him and he turned his head.

An alligator was heading directly toward them.

Ray knew how fast they were in the water, but they were deceptively quick on land. They were territorial. However, this one kept moving. Both men took off for the nearest tree. Jasper struggled but made it up to one of the middle branches. Ray had tried to sling his rifle over his shoulder, but the strap got tangled, and he had to ditch it. He had an easier time climbing, and soon the alligator was too far away to strike.

Instead, once the animal had reached the base of the tree, it did a slow revolution before it returned to the water's edge and slid effortlessly back into the murky depths.

Ray grabbed a cup from the cabinet, some green tea, and poured water. He placed the cup on a tray, along with apple sauce, and headed toward the stairs. Jennifer had been home from the hospital for about a week, and Ray had waited on her night and day. He didn't mind. It was just nice to have her back, even if it pained him to see her this way.

It had become too difficult for her to speak over the last few days. Ray reached over and took her hand and held it gently in his own. He could feel the bones in her fingers trying to squeeze his. He placed his other hand under the pillow, beneath her hand, and helped her to sit. She sipped the tea, and he spooned some apple sauce into her mouth. Afterward, he picked up the book on the nightstand and began reading from where he'd left off the previous day. When he saw her eyes begin to drift again, he closed the book without making a sound and exited the room.

Initially, the doctor told him that her prognosis looked hopeful, but things got worse exponentially. The only thing left to do was to make her as comfortable as possible. Ray placed the dishes in the sink. He watched the sunset for a moment through the kitchen window, grabbed a beer, and took a long pull. Then he cried. Not a lot; he didn't have much left, but some days he just got overwhelmed.

He went back upstairs in another half an hour, administered her pills, and changed her bedpan. Finally, he tucked her in for the evening. When he was almost at the doorway, he heard her speak.

Her voice was weak and strained. "Jasper."

"Do you want to play with those odds?" Ray asked without a hint of irony in his voice.

"That bad?" Jasper asked. He hadn't thought his plan of making a run for it was far-fetched, but Ray's response had given him doubts.

The alligator had returned and was sunning itself in between the tree and the water. It was smaller than it first appeared to be, but it was still sizable at about five and a half to six feet.

"This guy's aggressive. Alligators are territorial by nature. They mark off a spot and that's it. They'll defend it to the death, but once you're out of their territory, they leave you alone. They don't migrate unless they're finding a separate place to die."

Jasper's eyes lit up with a faint glint of hope.

"Even if that were true," Ray continued, "it might take days."

"Shit," Jasper said.

"This fella is different," Ray added. The respectful tone had caught Jasper off guard.

"So, what do we do?" Jasper asked.

"Go for the rifle," Ray replied and shifted his position, which revealed the handle of a knife on an ankle holster.

"What about that?" Jasper pointed to the blade.

"Do you want to try to stab an alligator?"

Jasper didn't say anything. "What do we do now?" he finally asked.

"I'm thinking," Ray said.

Jasper let his eyes drift back from the alligator. He jutted his chin toward the hole and shovel. "Why?"

"You should have been here *before* the funeral," Ray said.

"I already told you—"

"*What?*" Ray interjected, producing something from his pocket and throwing it at Jasper.

He caught it: a piece of balled-up paper. He unfolded it. A photograph, worn and yellowed, but Jasper had remembered the day it was taken. Jasper was maybe ten, standing in the backyard with his younger twin siblings, who'd just joined them.

"What could be more important than family?" Ray added.

"*Adopted* family," Jasper stated.

Ray was already up, with the knife in his hand.

He couldn't take it anymore. Whether Jasper understood or not was irrelevant. Ray negotiated all the branches like he'd been living in the treetops his whole life. The knife disappeared between Jasper's ribs, and Jasper let out a groan, as the wind was knocked out of him as well.

Ray held his brother for a moment and watched the light leave his eyes. He glanced down at the alligator and let the body fall. "Here you go," he said.

Ray could always return and fill the hole another time.

WITH GUN, DURING VIOLENCE

McManus took the punch, and his head snapped back. His brimmed hat had already tumbled to the floor. The sting of the blow was immediate, even though it hadn't been the first. However, a dull throbbing now accompanied it. He had begun to grind his teeth in anticipation, and now it sounded like a wood rasp at work.

Since the crash of '29, he'd had any and every job imaginable: digging ditches, working in an abattoir, and assisting Chao Kong Moon, an illusionist whose real name was Ira Silverberg. The latest gig had included running numbers for Hy Sugarman. Of course, his resume also included prizefighting. Mostly, he'd been a glorified sparring partner; Hell, it was really just an excuse for those who still had some greenbacks to watch the disenfranchised beat each other senseless.

As a result of his experience, he knew eyes naturally closed and muscles got tense in anticipation of the blow. It was what caused the whole process to seem worse than it was.

McManus lifted his head and winced. His right eye had practically swollen shut; the left wasn't much better. He wondered if he should have given it up so soon.

"All right, that's enough," Horst, the boss, the man in the corner said.

Sawyer, the man who had been busy enjoying his work restructuring McManus's face a little too much, gave Horst a sour look.

Horst walked from the corner of the room into the circle of light cast from overhead. He had on a pinstripe suit and a bowler hat a few sizes too big. Horst pulled a chair over, sat down, and lit a cigarette.

"Could I have one of those?" McManus asked.

Horst chuckled, ignored the request, took out a handkerchief, and wiped some of the blood off McManus's face.

McManus tried as best as he could to get comfortable in the chair to take his mind off the dull throbbing. It was difficult to make out every detail of the room since one of his eyes had lost its value. They were in a musty farmhouse. Sawyer had switched places with Horst and was now in the corner, whittling with his back up against the wall. He bit his lower lip as he scrutinized the blade gliding along the hickory he held in his other hand.

"Things could have gone smoother today," Horst said aloud, though it was really to himself.

McManus wanted to laugh but didn't. He hadn't heard such an understatement in a long time. In the beginning, things had gone very well for Boss Horst and Sawyer the Whittler. They had entered the bank, controlled the crowd like professionals, and dealt with the guards. Only one person tried to get out of line, and Sawyer had handled him.

The two criminals weren't greedy, and they didn't waste time. The problem had been The Continental Detective who'd been enjoying a stroll outside the bank. McManus had had the misfortune of entering the bank at the same time the criminals were exiting, so they grabbed him as a hostage and forced a standoff with the detective.

The detective, the getaway driver, and a few civilians had been killed during the melee; Horst and Sawyer had also lost some of the loot. Horst extinguished his cigarette. The sensation had returned to McManus's fingers, and he could touch the end of the rope binding his left wrist with his pinky.

"Now, here's the way that I see it," Horst said as he stood.

Sawyer continued to whittle.

"Do what you do best," Horst said to Sawyer and walked out from under the light.

Sawyer approached McManus with the knife out.

McManus tilted his head so he could look past Sawyer to where Horst had gone. In the far corner of the room, he could make out Horst uncovering the money from its hiding place. McManus smiled. Sawyer wrinkled his brow. McManus's hands were suddenly free from their bindings, and the derringer he kept near his groin was in his right hand.

Sawyer had begun to open his mouth but before he could make a sound, he had already been shot in the throat. Brilliant flashes of light erupted from the muzzle as McManus shot Horst in the back. McManus stood. He was still woozy, his balance compromised, so he took his time walking.

McManus rolled Horst's body over with the toe of his shoe.

"I guess we should have taken another hostage," Horst uttered.

McManus reached down and took the pack of cigarettes from Horst's breast pocket.

FAILURE DRILL

The man "Jimmy Jangles" was manicured and smooth around the edges. Most of them looked the same. Sometimes, there would be an outlier in the group who bucked the trend, but they almost all seemed to be a variation of the same archetype: below average height, thin, prescription glasses, and khaki pants. Other variables changed. Some were bald, others balding, and some brought gifts.

On the circuit, they were known as "Schmoes", men who paid female bodybuilders to participate in illicit activities with them. It rarely included sex. Instead, it focused on deviant practices such as domination, arm wrestling, and others. There was even something called "lift and carry".

The man, whose real name was James Sylvester, social media handle "Jimmy Jangles," knocked a few times on the door. It wasn't even part of a motel chain. The place looked like it existed solely for trysts and drug deals. Even though Deacon knew the woman inside wouldn't reveal her face when she opened the door, he couldn't help but feel the rush of adrenalin in anticipation.

Deacon didn't know her identity, just the screen name "Hefty Smurf Love". The door opened, but she had been standing off to the side. Jimmy Jangles walked inside, and the door closed.

How many times had Deacon watched a similar scene transpire? He'd lost count. Deacon killed his coffee and crushed the Styrofoam cup. It was his third of the evening, but the caffeine didn't bother him. He'd started as a PI for a divorce lawyer, Alan Titlebaum, until the ex-husband of a former client attacked Titlebaum after the ex-husband had been displeased with the results of the proceedings. Though he'd fixed Titlebaum's deviated septum, the ex-husband left Titlebaum with a traumatic brain injury that prevented Titlebaum from resuming his practice once he'd physically healed. Deacon was out of a gig, but there were enough spurned people out there who'd hire him to get dirt on their significant others. Before long, Deacon had his own shop up and running, and the work flowed at a steady rate.

Deacon checked the time. Jangles had only been in there for a few minutes. Deacon needed them to be engaged in something worthwhile for the photos to do anything, so he figured he'd wait another few minutes.

Deacon scanned the radio before he found a classic rock station that had just begun to play "Lunatic Fringe" by Red Rider. He thought back to the events of earlier that day. Since Jangles' rendezvous with Hefty Smurf Love wasn't until that evening, Deacon decided to attend the bodybuilding competition earlier in the afternoon. Though it had been sanctioned by one of the major organizations, the event took place at a community college auditorium. The room had been overpowered by the smell of Ben

Gay and baby oil. Raincoat types were peppered in amongst a sea of Gold's Gym tank tops.

Most of the bodybuilders had retained their feminine features, but some were androgenous. One person looked like Ziggy Stardust on twenty thousand calories a day. Deacon hazarded a guess the steroids probably didn't help. He had found Jangles in the crowd, and though Deacon didn't know who Hefty Smurf Love was, it didn't stop him from making assumptions.

Deacon took a seat as the wellness category began. Next to him was a man who kept reviewing the program and discussing the finer points of the competition with the woman seated on the other side of him. Possibly, they had been on a date. The man didn't have the requisite look of a schmoe. Instead, he was probably just a connoisseur of the art form. He had the build of someone who might have been an amateur competitor in his youth. Deacon listened to the man comment about the event for a while but left before they could begin the physique category. However, on his way out, he overheard the man mention how later this month the college's theater department was going to start a week-long run of *Godspell*.

Deacon found a burger joint nearby. He still had another two hours before Jangles and Hefty Smurf Love were set to rendezvous at the motel. He took the time to go over his notes from his meeting with his client, Sy Carruthers.

"I represent Mary Sylvester, soon to be Mary O'Connor."

Carruthers had sat in the guest chair in Deacon's office as if Carruthers had been holding court with a visiting dignitary. Carruthers had looked out of place.

The office wasn't in disrepair or anything, but Deacon had kept the same layout and furniture from when he'd first became the tenant. Suggesting the room had been outdated would have been kind.

Carruthers was overweight but not significantly, and his tailored suit hid most of it. Deacon hadn't recognized the man, but he'd heard the name before. Carruthers worked exclusively for the two-comma clientele, and he'd been known to represent some heavy hitters. Deacon had therefore been curious to know how Carruthers came to be in Deacon's office. They ran in completely different circles. Carruthers had revealed he and Mr. Titlebaum had had a mutual acquaintance, who'd spoken highly of Deacon's work.

"Initially, Mary had wanted to take care of it a different way," Carruthers had said. *Hell hath no fury*.

Later, Deacon would discover Mary O'Connor had a first cousin, Lionel Adams, who ran one of the more powerful crime syndicates in the city.

"However, I managed to convince her to settle it in a court of law. She's going to sue Mr. Sylvester for divorce," Carruthers said.

Deacon thought about whether he should get involved. If he opened the door to Carruthers, there was no closing it. Though Carruthers advised litigation this time, who was to say it would always be that way? Deacon looked around the office again. He could continue nickel and diming it and take photos for angered cuckolds. If he started working for Carruthers, he might end up like Titlebaum or worse.

Still ... Deacon looked at Carruthers in his camel hair coat, sharkskin suit, leather attache case, and knew his mind had already been made up.

"When do I start?" Deacon asked.

Carruthers gave Deacon some email correspondence between Mr. Sylvester, aka Jimmy Jangles, and Hefty Smurf Love.

"They're going to meet after she participates in a competition."

Carruthers stood, which indicated their meeting had ended. Aside from some preliminary questions, Deacon had barely spoken.

"Address of the motel is in here as well," Carruthers said.

He gave Deacon an envelope with the first half of his payment and a phone number where Carruthers could be reached. The rest of the money would be conferred upon delivery of the photos, the lewder the better. Before Deacon could ask any more questions, Carruthers had left.

The memory gone, Deacon finished his burger, and checked the time. The motel was only ten minutes away, so he got apple pie for dessert. Now, he sat in the driver's seat with his Sony CyberShot and a telephoto lens ready to go. He waited until the next song, "Eye of the Tiger" by Survivor, had finished.

Earlier, he had gone to the front desk, claimed he was James Sylvester, gave the room number, and said he'd misplaced his keycard. The kid working the counter, probably a student at the community college, barely acknowledged the request. Long hair that hadn't been washed in a long time came down to his neck. The kid looked stoned, or he'd just awoken from a coma. Maybe, he was going to portray Judas in *Godspell*?

However, without hesitating, the kid put a replacement card in the machine and made a copy. Deacon thought the kid would hand him the card along with a clever remark about not losing this one, but the kid stayed quiet. Deacon thanked him and tipped him a few bucks.

The keycard opened the door.

Hefty Smurf Love and Jimmy Jangles were on the bed. She had him in a headlock. She was wearing workout clothes and a cape. Jangles was shirtless and wore tights. They both looked like professional wrestlers. The match stopped when they saw Deacon.

His sudden appearance in the room startled them and they both started to raise Hell, but he had already taken at least forty pictures. It would have been better if they were in flagrante delicto, but these would be good enough. The threat of releasing the photos to the public would tip the scales in Mary O'Connor's favor.

Both Hefty and Jangles had broken their embrace and were now issuing threats. Deacon had what he needed and turned to go. The whole thing had only taken a few moments.

Another man entered the room. He was thick. Deacon remembered Titlebaum had once used the phrase "prison big" and it seemed to fit this mystery man. The guy was in an overcoat and wore a ski mask. He also carried a silenced handgun. Tattoos peeked from underneath his coat sleeves. He shot Sylvester/Jangles twice in the chest and once in the forehead in a fluid motion. Deacon froze, but Hefty Smurf Love had started to scream. The man with the weapon lowered it and left.

On his way out, he spoke to Deacon. "Mary changed her mind."

THREE LITTLE PIGS

"Did it say Ice Cube's a pimp?" asked Floyd and smirked.

Angela stared at him. It wasn't a look of anger or confusion, but one of pity.

Floyd was sitting in a chair in front of the mirror, which served as the makeup station before showtime. Except for the head, he was already wearing his costume of the pig who'd built his house out of bricks. When they'd been given the costumes, each had simply been tagged Pig 1, 2, and 3. However, Floyd had suggested they *embrace* the story. He had been an actor at one point and said it would help with his motivation if he could be the final pig from the story.

Neither Delaney nor Byron cared, so they'd agreed.

Floyd's blonde hair was disheveled, since he hadn't showered that morning, and he continued to sport a wry smile on his face, which those who knew him either grew to love or hate.

It wasn't difficult to figure out where Angela stood on the matter.

"No, it didn't," she said dryly.

She hadn't known Floyd was referring to the song "A Good Day" by Ice Cube, but she probably assumed it was something esoteric. Floyd had once introduced himself, Delaney, and Byron as Whitman, Price, and Haddad, three of the contestants from the film *The Running Man*, an Arnold Schwarzenegger vehicle based on a Stephen King book about a futuristic game show. It didn't matter to Floyd whether anyone ever got any of his references, and it had gotten him into trouble more than once, but he didn't care.

Angela had come into the trailer, excited to have just seen The Goodyear Blimp, and she had wanted to share her joy with them. The fact she was already dressed as Princess Jasmine only added to the surreal quality of the scene.

The drugs probably exacerbated everything too.

Angela turned around and slammed the door behind her. Delaney assumed that was probably the last time she would voluntarily enter their trailer. He watched Floyd spill out a few more pills from the prescription bottle into his hand, quaff them, and chase them with coffee.

One of the savvy veterans who'd portrayed Dopey for the last five years had suggested Adderall.

"Trust me, after three days you'll need it," the guy said.

His name was Reginald, and he'd begun just like the three of them had: in costumes. As a little person, the roles he was offered weren't varied but eventually, he worked his way up to being able to perform without having to wear "the full getup", as he called it.

Now, as Dopey, he only had to change clothes and add the hat.

As a community college student, Byron was able to get his hands on a steady supply of pills. He had taken the job at the theme park to help offset tuition. Like Floyd, Byron was indifferent about the job. He would rather be doing something else, but this beat flipping burgers. At about six feet, he was the tallest and thinnest of the group, and probably weighed about one-thirty in the costume.

At first, their supervisor, Heather was going to 86 Byron for being too tall, but word from up high suggested it might be better to have some more variety between the three pigs, other than their type of dwelling.

Delaney, the final member of the group, was also the oldest. He was a high school English teacher whose divorce had set him back and he needed the money. He'd known Heather through a family connection, so the summer job was his if he wanted it. He was the only one who voiced his displeasure with the work, and the fear he'd be discovered by one of his students. But at the end of the day, the alimony checks needed to be paid and, as Byron once said, it was better than flipping burgers.

The door to the trailer opened, Byron walked in, threw his backpack on the floor, and retrieved his costume from the wardrobe rack. "Sorry, fellas," he said. "Physics is killing me."

"No worries," Floyd responded and drank more coffee. "Just don't let Heather catch you again."

Byron exhaled and began changing. If he was caught arriving late again, it would be another infraction and result in his pay being docked. Heather was cool about a lot of things, but she wouldn't look the other way regarding breaking the rules.

"Did I miss anything?" Byron asked as he pulled up his lower half.

"The Goodyear Blimp," Floyd said.

"By the way," Delaney began, "it's 'what did the blimp read' and not say. Blimps can't speak."

"Duly noted," Floyd stated.

Floyd wasn't the only one who'd rubbed people the wrong way with his behavior. As a practicing English teacher, it was virtually impossible for Delaney not to correct any grammatical or syntactical errors. After Delaney had recognized it was an annoying habit, he had made a conscious effort to address it. Floyd still didn't care about his pop culture references, though.

Someone knocked on the door.

"Come in," Delaney said.

The door opened.

"You guys almost ready?"

Constantine stood in the doorway in his full big bad wolf outfit, with the head already in place. Technically, an employee could get written up if they were visible out of costume, but Constantine never had to worry about that.

"We'll be there in ten," Delaney replied.

"See you there."

Constantine shut the door.

Floyd had once compared the three of them to the lead characters from the film *M*A*S*H*, alcoholic surgeons during the Korean War who frequently broke the rules to stay sane during a crazy time. Floyd suggested Constantine would be the equivalent of Robert Duvall's character, Major Frank Burns, a religious zealot who had no sense of humor. While Constantine wasn't a religious zealot by any stretch, he did take his job at the park very seriously. He was the only one of the four of them who worked there without an ulterior motive. He truly enjoyed bringing smiles to the faces of children. He had a son at home with special needs, and he frequently took his kid to work with him. When Constantine wasn't working at the park, or as a plumber, he was a volunteer sheriff's deputy.

"We should get going," Delaney said.

By this time, Byron had gotten fully dressed and Floyd had finished his coffee.

"What's the rush?" Floyd asked. "We've still got a few minutes."

Floyd was right about them not needing to be on the clock quite yet, but Constantine had suggested they all hit their marks a few minutes early, so they would never be late for starting time.

Constantine had begun to complain to Delaney about the group's attitude, but Delaney had withheld it from them. "No rush," Delaney said.

Floyd crushed his Styrofoam cup, threw it in the trash, and placed on his head to complete the costume. "Alright, let's do this."

They only had to do five shows a day, but they also had to walk around the park and mingle with the guests for at least an hour. Constantine would never do less than two hours, and at one point Heather was going to increase the time limit, but Delaney and Byron had persuaded her to leave it at one.

Now, Floyd and Delaney sat in their street clothes at a picnic table near their trailer. The park was closing, so they could afford to be in their "civilian attire", as Constantine would have referred to it.

Both Floyd and Delaney had large sodas, which Floyd had spiked with mini bottles of rum he'd pilfered from one of the minibar supply carts. Floyd would occasionally get shifts working as a bellhop at one of the park resorts. Occasionally, he'd fill in for any other job they needed. He'd frequently help himself to the amenities. No matter how many times Delaney said the hotel probably had surveillance going, Floyd would suggest it was just a fringe benefit, and if they saw fit to garnish his wages, so be it.

Byron went home after the final show ended. He'd be up all night again, wrestling with physics concepts that were just out of his grasp.

"You know," Floyd began, then stopped speaking, and watched a golf cart pass their table.

Behind the wheel was one of the park security guards making his weekly deposit. Next to him, on the passenger seat of the golf cart, was a strong box.

"How much you think he's got in there?" Floyd after the guard had left their immediate vicinity.

"I don't know," Delaney said. "A few grand?"

"That's what I was thinking," Floyd said. "I watched *Heat* the other night," he added.

"No," Delaney replied.

"You don't even know what—"

"Fine. What were you going to say?"

Floyd paused, then finally asked, "How difficult would it be?"

"Look," Delaney said, "let's just forget it."

"You think Fred Sanford is going to do something?" Floyd asked and pointed in the direction the guard had gone.

"We're not robbing the park!" Delaney declared through gritted teeth.

Neither man spoke for a moment.

"How much of your paycheck goes to her?" Floyd's tone had softened, but the words still had bite.

Delaney took another drink and slid the cup in front of Floyd. "Hit me again," he said. He watched Floyd dump in another mini bottle. Delaney took the drink back, took a healthy slug, and spoke. "Too much."

"OK, so let's change that," Floyd said. He sat up straighter in his chair, recognizing he had begun to hook Delaney.

"No one gets hurt," Delaney advised.

"No one gets hurt. We won't even have loaded weapons."

Both men killed their drinks.

"Let me come up with a plan tonight," Floyd said. "And we'll both tell Byron tomorrow after his project is finished."

"Sounds good."

First, they made certain Byron was interested. It took some convincing, but like Delaney when Byron had been reminded about student loans, that was all. Floyd had prepared a very loose presentation. He said a few things were going for them. The first was that the typical guards weren't ex-commando special forces looking to recreate their glory days. Odds were they were counting down the minutes until they could retire on a pension of some sort. Not to mention, it was theme park cash they were transporting, not legal tender. The brass would know it was an inside job, but Floyd argued they wouldn't be able to prove anything unless one of them was caught. He'd be able to get some replica guns from a special effects friend. On the day in question, they would finish their final shift, leave the park, return, and knock over the golf cart when it went to make the deposit. Floyd said it would take him about a week to put everything together.

They all agreed the following Friday would be the day. The days leading up to it flew by. Except for a few conversations about how they would launder the money, no one brought it up. Both Delaney and Byron already knew how they would spend their portions. Floyd seemed to be genuinely excited just to participate.

When Byron asked him why he was so gung-ho on committing the heist, Floyd responded with, "The action is the juice." He said it was from the film *Heat*, but the significance had been lost on both Delaney and Byron.

The morning of the caper, there were no surprises. Angela hadn't stopped by since Floyd had asked about the message on the side of the blimp but as usual, Constantine was at the door fifteen minutes before showtime. The guys indulged him as they usually did, then waited until a minute to showtime before arriving on set. Delaney had again suggested they get there early, but Floyd said nothing could be out of the ordinary.

"It might draw suspicion, like 'Meinertzhagen's Haversack'." He went on to explain it was a strategy of deception, employed to make it seem like nothing was amiss. "It was on an episode of *Silicon Valley*."

Delaney and Byron both nodded. Neither of them got any of Floyd's references, but they humored him, nonetheless. The performances went off without a hitch. In between shows, the three of them made sure to circulate through the park for their mandatory hour, while Constantine almost set another record. At the end of the final performance, the three of them returned to the trailer to drop off their costumes.

From there, they would take their own cars and meet up at the mall nearby. Floyd had already parked one of the laundry trucks from the resort in the mall parking lot. Byron and Delaney would get in the back with clean clothes, and they would return to the park. They'd set up and intercept the security guard during the stretch of his route, just after his last pickup and before his drop off at the office.

Before they got into the back of the truck, Floyd gave them their replica pistols. Even up close, they looked legitimate. Delaney checked the clip to make sure it was empty.

"Relax," Floyd said. "I didn't even load it with blanks. We don't need it."

Delaney and Byron got in the back of the truck, Floyd shut the door and got behind the wheel. Within five minutes, they were back in the park. All three of them wore bandanas over their noses and mouths, with the hoods of their sweatshirts pulled up high.

Floyd waited until the coast was clear before getting them from the back.

Delaney checked the time. If there hadn't been any deviations in the schedule, the golf cart would be approaching within the next few minutes. Each of them found blind spots near the road so they could brace the security guard as soon as he crossed the point of no return.

The park was always eerie at this time of day. All the rides had been shut down, all the patrons and most of the staff had gone home. The occasional conversation would carry from the parking lot, people saying their goodbyes, but otherwise there was nothing.

The three men dealt with last-second jitters. Floyd, however, had instructed them to think about how no one would get hurt, the money could easily be laundered through the park, and they wouldn't have to worry anymore about alimony or tuition.

In another moment, they saw the golf cart approach. The guard behind the wheel was middle-aged with white hair and a walrus-style mustache. Once, Floyd had remarked the guy looked like Wilford Brimley. This time, Delaney had gotten the reference, but Byron hadn't.

Floyd walked to the center of the road with his hand up, and Wilford slowed down.

"Hep you with somethin'?" Wilford inquired.

"Sorry," Floyd said and pulled the weapon. He held it sideways at first, showing the profile so Wilford could get a good look at it.

Delaney and Byron scrambled from their spots and joined Floyd.

"What—" Wilford started to say, then slumped forward onto the horn.

The sound reverberated around the now empty park and Wilford shot back into his seat.

"Jesus Christ!" he yelled.

"We need to call an ambulance!" Delaney said.

"Why?" Floyd said.

"Wilford's having a heart attack!" Delaney spat out angrily

Wilford looked at Delaney with a furrowed brow.

"What's your name?" Floyd said.

"Jesse," replied Wilford.

"Jesse, are you having a heart attack?"

"No. I get dizzy spells sometimes."

"Good. Now that we've gotten that out of the way, can we move it?" Floyd said.

Part two of the plan was to leave the guard by the side of the road, take the golf cart back to the entrance where they'd stashed a dolly, and move the safe back into the truck. They'd have all night to go to work on it, following instructions from schematics Floyd had found on the internet.

Byron went to take Wilford/Jesse by the elbow and escort him from the cart when he was hit in the chest with a projectile. It had been a rolled-up t-shirt. Both Floyd and Delaney looked down the stretch of road to see Constantine fifty feet away, sprinting toward them, and holding a t-shirt gun. He still wore the lower half of his Big Bad Wolf costume, but the upper half was missing.

"Forget this," Delaney said and started to run.

Constantine stopped, aimed the t-shirt gun, and fired again. The rolled-up t-shirt hit Delaney square in the back and knocked him to the ground. Constantine was only a few feet away now, and Floyd turned the weapon around so he held the barrel. When Constantine got within range, Floyd swung the piece like a hammer, but Constantine easily dodged it. He swung the t-shirt gun and hit Floyd in the chin. Floyd's head snapped back, and his legs gave way. He could taste the copper of blood flowing from his split lip.

Constantine stood over him and put a foot on his chest.

Floyd slid his bandana down.

"Figures," Constantine said after he saw who it was. He jutted with his chin toward one of the other fallen bodies.

"That'd be Byron?"

"And Delaney," Floyd said.

Constantine suddenly had a pained look on his face. A siren grew louder in the distance.

"I'd stay down if I were you," Constantine called out to the other two who had begun to stir. He took his foot off Floyd's chest.

"How ... you?" Floyd managed before a coughing fit erupted.

"I trained with the SEALs back in '93," Constantine replied.

The last thought Floyd had before he passed out was how similar the situation was to the ending of the film *Heat*.

JUNK PAPER

"I can't keep overlooking these infractions."

Martin Chalmers resembled a ventriloquist's dummy who had come to life, including a wan complexion, dull features, and an ill-fitting suit. An oversized jar of antacid tablets was on his desk, and he popped a handful of them every few minutes. He cracked them between his teeth and the residue coated his tongue. The rest of the office was overrun with folders and loose papers, but Chalmers had a system and knew where everything was located.

Simon Orlov, the recipient of the lecture, didn't care for Chalmers, but Simon knew he'd need to hear the man out regardless. Simon looked like he'd been fashioned from a piece of scrap metal. Even at an advanced age, there was a ferocity about him that would have intimidated most people. His snow-white hair was kept in a crew cut, the same look he'd had when he was in the service.

Chalmers ran the assisted living facility of which Simon was a resident. Simon had in fact broken almost all the rules Chalmers had listed previously, including a few he hadn't mentioned. Simon's sister Jan was on the board of directors, so Simon knew he was above reproach. Still, he couldn't poke the bear too many times, so he would listen to Chalmers hem and haw and talk about things like decency and respect.

Simon wondered if he had any painkillers left and realized he might have to grease that orderly, Rock, to let him pilfer the dispensary for some Schedule II goods.

"I know things haven't been easy. There's been unpleasantness," Chalmers said and sighed. He popped a few more tablets.

That was the way he usually ended his sermons, so Simon knew the man had finished. Chalmers never talked about the difficulties Simon had had in adjusting after combat; Chalmers always used euphemisms. Simon shook his head in agreement a few times and tried to look as forlorn as he could. He gripped the wheels of his wheelchair, backed away from the desk, executed a quick 180, and left the room.

Chalmers helped himself to a few more antacid tablets; most of them were placebos, but they still helped to put him at ease, especially when his anxiety was going off the rails. He'd spent the last few days trying to come up with a way to address the problems he was having with Simon Orlov. Restriction of privileges, punishments, nothing seemed to work. The man had spent time in a prisoner-of-war camp, so really there was nothing Chalmers could do within the rulebook that would phase Orlov. With Jan Orlov on the board of directors, Chalmers' hands were essentially tied on how far he could push things. Chalmers had had plans to climb the ladder, and Simon Orlov stood in his way.

A BUREAUCRATIC DESIRE FOR REVENGE

The man would have to be dealt with.

Sistrunk's Iron Works operated as a garage and salvage yard, but they also did repossession, collection, and occasionally some second-floor work. Felonies weren't really their thing, but the owner, Emmitt "Too Sharp" Sistrunk, was looking to expand his empire. So, when Martin Chalmers called and inquired about getting rid of a resident of a retirement home, Sistrunk jumped at the chance.

Chalmers had said he had gotten Sistrunk's number from a former colleague who'd used Sistrunk and his crew to collect an outstanding debt. The colleague had suggested Sistrunk would be discreet.

"Uh, so, this is a tricky situation," Chalmers said.

"Don't worry. We know what we're doing," Sistrunk replied.

Sistrunk was a barrel-chested man with male pattern baldness and a trimmed beard. He wore flannel no matter the temperature. Both men took the opportunity of the ensuing silence to indulge themselves. Chalmers ingested some more antacid tablets, and Sistrunk placed a sizeable chunk of Kodiak chewing tobacco in the gumline between his teeth and lower lip.

"I've got someone I can put on this, starting tomorrow," Sistrunk said and spat a brown wad into a Dixie cup. Sistrunk thought of Timothy Jacobs; the kid still needed some seasoning, but he was turning out to be a decent employee.

"Orlov goes outside in the afternoon for about an

hour if the weather's nice," Chalmers told him. "Otherwise, he leaves sporadically," he added.

"'Scuse me?"

"He doesn't go outside often," Chalmers replied and reached for more antacid. One of these days, he'd have to make another appointment for a GI doctor, but he could wait until Simon Orlov had been removed from the picture.

There was another lull in the conversation.

"What happens now?" Chalmers asked.

"We need a down payment of a third upfront," Sistrunk explained and quickly tried to come up with a sum that would be right in the sweet spot. He didn't want to price himself out, but he also didn't want to lowball and sabotage the potential to grow the business. Who knew whether this opportunity might lead to something else?

"That'll be $3000," Sistrunk finally said and held his breath.

Chalmers waited a moment, as if he were scrutinizing the number, before he answered. "That's fine," he said.

Chalmers had done some research too. He had gone to a public library and looked up contract killing. He didn't want to inadvertently leave any traces on his computer at the office. On *Wikipedia*, it suggested an average price was about $15,000. For $9000, Chalmers was getting a sweetheart deal, although he tried to rid himself of the thought that "you get what you pay for".

"Cash, check, or money order?" Sistrunk inquired.

"I'm sorry—"

Sistrunk cut off Chalmers before he could continue. "We operate as a salvage and restoration facility. Make it out to Sistrunk Iron Works and, if anyone asks, we're restoring a car for you."

A beat went by before Chalmers responded with a mouthful of half-chewed tablets. "OK." He didn't want to argue with Sistrunk about how ridiculous it would seem for Chalmers to restore a car when he didn't even have a license, but he'd come up with something. The important thing was to take care of Orlov before Chalmers started to have second thoughts.

"I'll get you a money order today."

"Great."

"Also, it has to look like a robbery."

"Can do."

"And we have other residents, so no firearms."

Sistrunk spit out another wad of tobacco. "Anything else?"

"No, that's it. Thank—"

But Sistrunk had already hung up the phone. Sistrunk felt exhilarated at the possibility of developing his business, and Chalmers immediately reached for the antacid, and began to think about where he could siphon three grand. He also made a mental note to look up whether Orlov had an insurance policy and beneficiaries.

Simon took his time slowly rolling along the pathway. He enjoyed the chill in the air as winter slowly gave way to spring. Fewer people were outside, and he relished the solitude. He took his time watching birds fly and squirrels forage. Something was amiss though, and he picked up on it. When he was in 'Nam, some in his unit thought he'd had a preternatural sense for sniffing out ambushes. The ability hadn't left him and now, almost sixty years later, he used it again in the courtyard of the retirement home.

"You can come out," he said.

A moment passed before a lanky kid with a shaved head and a bull ring through his nose emerged from behind the main building. The kid's brow was furrowed, as if he'd been trying to figure out how Simon had made him. The kid held a bicycle chain in one hand that swung by his knee. The kid stopped walking when he got a few feet away.

"What's your name?" Simon asked.

"Timothy," the kid said.

"How old are you?"

"Thirty-one. We playing twenty questions?"

"No," Simon replied.

"I'm sorry," the kid said. He swung the chain.

Simon wore fingerless gloves to help maneuver the wheelchair. He caught the end of the bike chain in his left hand. The kid hadn't expected this. Timothy thought the old man would soil himself and succumb easily. The last thing he expected was that the old man would fight back. The fact he was currently playing tug-of-war with a geriatric in a wheelchair had blown his mind.

Simon pulled the chain and Timothy lurched toward him. Simon connected with a right cross that rattled Timothy's teeth. The kid was unconscious before he hit the ground.

"Maybe you could have mentioned he was Special Forces?" Sistrunk suggested and sprayed bits of tobacco as he spoke.

Timothy Jacobs had a broken jaw and was going to have to eat from a straw for the next few months; so much for grooming new talent. On the other end of the phone, the sound of a lid coming unscrewed could be heard as Chalmers opened the seal on another jar of antacid tablets.

Chalmers could have reminded Sistrunk that Simon Orlov was a senior who had been Special Forces half a century ago, but he chose another tact. "What do we do now?"

Sistrunk stopped speaking. The dream of expanding his empire wasn't snuffed out. He needed to resuscitate it again. "I've got someone else in mind," he said, "but I'll need another deposit; double it this time."

"Fine."

They both hung up the phone. Chalmers had managed to divert some of the funds from the pension account. This time around, he could tap the 401K; he was good with numbers, after all. This was too important. He popped another few tablets and chased them with root beer.

Patrick Vanderhicks Bar & Grill hadn't served food in over a decade, but the neon sign advertising the grill had remained unchanged. It was the type of place where the jukebox only played sad ballads, smoking was still allowed indoors, and the Off-Track Betting circuit played on the bar's only television. It was definitely the type of place forbidden to Cleon Odom, as it was a clear violation of his parole. However, he wasn't going to have any drinks or fraternize with undesirables. He just enjoyed watching the races and imagining who he would have bet on had he still had the chance.

Watching the harness races on closed-circuit television brought him solace in a way almost nothing else could. Besides, it wasn't like his PO would make a surprise visit. Cleon's PO, Maria Fago, wasn't a hardass. She was still an idealistic holdover from a graduate school out west, someone truly looking to make a difference. She would cut Cleon some slack, but Cleon also wouldn't give her any reasons to violate his parole.

Cleon had been working on a cup of coffee and a tuna melt he'd brought with him from the diner when the phone rang behind the bar. Doreen, whose shift had begun fifteen minutes earlier, cleared her throat and picked up the phone. A two-pack-a-day smoker, her voice sounded like sandpaper as she said the name of the establishment.

She listened and placed both the base and receiver on the bar next to Cleon. "For you," she said.

Cleon wiped his hand on a napkin and picked up the receiver. "Yeah," he said.

"It's Emmitt," Sistrunk said.

There was silence as Cleon took another bite.

"I wouldn't bother you if it wasn't life or death," Sistrunk stated.

"I left that behind," Cleon said.

Sistrunk knew he should be empathetic but that wouldn't get him anywhere. Instead, he decided to play his trump card right off the bat. "Look, this thing comes off ..."

Cleon took another bite and chased it with some coffee.

Sistrunk knew since Cleon hadn't hung up the phone he would keep listening.

"We can find out if Mr. Ham Sandwich has sired any kids."

There it was. Cleon hadn't responded, but Sistrunk knew he'd hooked him.

"A special project," Sistrunk said. "Swing by the office, so I can tell you in person."

"Be there in forty-five minutes." Cleon hung up the phone.

Sistrunk had looked the same as Cleon had remembered, just a few more age lines. He was still stout, though. The ink tattooing his knuckles with "Too Sharp" had begun to fade a little. Sistrunk thought Cleon had looked more put together, as if his time in the joint had allowed him to prosper.

Cleon had been the best debt collector Sistrunk had ever employed. In what had been the golden age, as Sistrunk remembered it, you could break the bones in a man's hand if he'd been delinquent and not have to worry about frivolous lawsuits.

"Silver Star '73 single-handedly took out a platoon in the Hà Tĩnh province."

Sistrunk had been upset at the setback and intrigued at the same time, so he did some research on Simon Orlov. Sistrunk was nearing the end of his recitation about the man's achievements. "This is a man who knocks people unconscious with a single blow," Sistrunk said, quoting from one of his favorite films, *Diggstown*.

Years ago, he and Cleon would pick up a bottle of Crown Royal and watch a VHS of *Diggstown*. They did this so often, the magnetic cohesion on the tape had started to disintegrate.

"So, it's open season?" Cleon asked. He had already checked with Mr. Ham Sandwich's owner/trainer Barry Fitz-Hume. The man said there were a few foals who he'd sell for the right price.

"Like old times," Sistrunk said.

He snapped open the Kodiak lid, offered it to Cleon, who passed, and placed another dollop between his teeth and gum. They revisited some more history for a few minutes before Anderson gave Cleon the details of the assignment.

"The Fulcrum."

That had been one of Simon's nicknames for as long as he could remember. Besides his ability to detect pitfalls, he had the ability to pivot and adapt to any situation. For example, he could still afford to abuse the Dilaudid he'd gotten from Rock before he had to worry about going through withdrawal if he didn't take it. He turned the corner and continued down the path near the courtyard.

This thing with Chalmers was approaching the point of no return, but it hadn't gotten there quite yet. He'd see if Petra the "relaxation therapist" could make another visit now that he'd gotten a new supply of Yellow Jackets from the gas station near the highway exit.

He continued to roll along the path, taking in the serene quality of the surroundings.

He'd read an article recently about how STDs were on the rise in retirement communities since more people were remaining active. He made a mental note to ask Rock to pick him up some protection the next time he had the chance. Jasmine was a professional, but Simon left little to chance. His days of going "Bareback Jones" were over.

Simon ambled into the courtyard until he got to his spot. The grounds were well maintained and uniform in design, save for a single oak tree set off from an arrangement of tables and benches. Simon would leave the paved walkway, find solace under the shadows of the branches, and let his mind wander. Sometimes, he'd revisit memories, but most of the time he'd spend time with Mr. Puff.

Mr. Puff was a stray cat who visited the grounds; an outdoor cat who lived nearby. Mr. Puff was large for a cat, the size of a rat terrier, really, and stayed away or hissed at anyone who approached—everyone that is, except for Simon. Typically, Simon would come to a full stop, whistle once, Mr. Puff would come running, and jump onto Simon's lap. Together, they would stay under the tree for about an hour, until lunch. Simon kept waiting for the axe to fall, for Chalmers or someone else to say that due to a complaint or change in policy, Mr. Puff would be forbidden from the grounds. However, so far, no one had said anything. Eventually, Mr. Puff would leave as silently as he'd arrived.

For now, though, the two of them enjoyed the brisk day.

Cleon was able to secure a position as a volunteer at the facility two nights a week, which was all he thought he would need to get the lay of the land and figure out the best way to deal with Orlov. He'd had a brief orientation when he'd arrived, but he was about to start his first shift. He had taken a seat in one of the armchairs in the lobby, affixed the visitor's sticker to his shirt, and put in his earbuds. The main riff to "Amygdala" by Slow Green Thing had just kicked in when his guide showed. Since Cleon was the only person in the lobby, the orderly walked over with no hesitation.

"Cleon?" the orderly asked. She had a nameplate on her shirt which read S. Rock.

"Yeah," Cleon said and stood up.

"Name's Scarlett. Nice to meet you."

"Likewise."

"Follow me," Rock instructed, and began walking.

Cleon turned off his music and caught up.

"There's no better way to show you how to do this," Rock said. She handed Cleon some ear plugs and began to insert some.

Cleon hesitated for a moment and stared at them.

"I'd suggest you put them in," Rock said.

He did so. The earplugs had just begun to expand in Cleon's ears as Rock opened the door, stepped through the threshold, motioned Cleon to follow, and shut the door behind them. Even with the protection, the operatic singing was oppressive, so much that

Cleon could *feel* the sound. The voice belonged to an elderly woman with a frail body. She probably stood just a little over five feet tall, and may have weighed ninety pounds, but her vocal ability was on the level with a contralto a few hundred pounds heavier. She had assumed an awkward position, like she'd been afflicted with a degenerative disorder, and was delivering her vocals with so much passion, her throat muscles were undulating.

Cleon was mesmerized and stood a few feet away, continuing to marvel. Rock hadn't paid the singer any attention. Instead, she had begun to change the sheets and straighten the room.

"Hey!" Rock said.

Cleon broke away from staring. "Huh?"

"Help me with this," Rock instructed and gestured toward the far side of the bed.

Cleon was about to ask about the room's occupant when the woman suddenly stopped singing. Cleon looked over again. The woman was like a statue, stuck in a pose that didn't suggest any particular emotion, but there was still an intensity. Her eyes started out into space, but her cataracts had obscured the pupils of her eyes.

"Her name is Hanrahan," Rock said. "Louise Hanrahan. It's like clockwork. She starts singing around four and goes for exactly forty minutes. You can set your watch to it." Rock finished replacing the fitted sheet, turned, put her hands on her hips, and looked at Ms. Hanrahan the way a museum curator might appraise a sculpture. She undid the band holding the elderly woman's hair in a ponytail and redid it.

"Anything else?" Cleon asked.

"Not in here."

Rock led the way and Cleon followed. They checked on a few more residents, and Rock told stories of having to go into the air conditioning ventilation to constantly retrieve a former tunnel rat.

"There was stuff in those vents you wouldn't believe."

Among the items Rock discovered were medication samples, stuffed animals, decayed flowers. They finished making the rounds. Rock was going to get a blueberry muffin from the deli on the corner; she invited Cleon to join her, but he passed. Before she left, she confirmed he would indeed accept the position and return for work the following evening.

Cleon said he would. Outside, they went in separate directions. Cleon put on his headphones and cued up Slow Green Thing. Rock went to Lee Anne's Deli on the corner and ordered "The Bomb," a specialty 14" sandwich with multiple meats and cheeses. It would be lunch for the next day as well. Rock returned to the facility and sat outside, on one of the benches. She put in her earbuds and rested the plastic bag with dinner on the seat next to her. First, she'd take care of some business, then she'd dine. She dialed the number and waited.

"Bob's Gold Rush."

"Reggie, it's Scarlett."

"Give me a second," Reggie said. "Alright, what do you have?"

Rock went through the latest acquisitions. Anytime she had found something, she would legitimately look for the item's true owner, whether it had intrinsic value or not. When no one claimed it, the item would go into the Lost & Found box at the reception desk.

During her first year, Rock realized once an item made it into the box, it was never claimed. So that she wouldn't feel conflicted, she created a system of checks and balances. Items would only make it to the pawn shop if it hadn't been claimed after the second email blast went unanswered.

Rock hadn't made a killing by any stretch, but it was a stream of passive income, and the way she saw it there were no victims. She finished by describing the dimensions of a dragonfly broach, waited for Reggie to confirm the details, hung up and enjoyed her sandwich.

"The M18A1 Claymore."

Duke Ragnar held up the device, laid it on the table, and took a healthy drag from his Marlboro Red. Timothy Jacobs started to nod, but pain immediately flooded his body. He shut his eyes, clenched his teeth, and waited for the moment to pass. He wanted to lean forward, put his forehead on the table, and just go to sleep. He couldn't do that though, and the only thing that made him feel better was knowing that now he'd be able to pay that old man back. Timothy opened his eyes and waited for Ragnar to continue.

"A directional, anti-personnel mine that can be activated by you or your target."

"OK."

Ragnar took another drag, extinguished his cigarette, and lit another. Ragnar had a beard that practically hung down to his sternum, and Timothy couldn't understand how the man was able to smoke without singeing himself.

"So, you lay it down, front toward the enemy," Ragnar said and took another healthy drag.

Timothy lifted the case, which looked like an old metal lunchbox. Front toward enemy had been stenciled on the side. "OK."

"You depress the clicker, and it ignites the C-4 explosive, which disperses several hundred ball-bearings." Ragnar held up the clicker, which had been attached to the box from a wire.

Timothy placed the case back on the table and swallowed. The GI doctor suggested he would always have problems with certain—how did the doctor put it?—"elements of mastication". The pain set in, but it was blunted by an image in his head of the old man on the receiving end of several hundred ball-bearings traveling, according to Ragnar, with speeds up to four thousand feet per second.

"I'll take it."

Mr. Puff had just departed and Simon brushed cat hair from his pants. He gripped the wheels of his chair to execute a turn, but changed his mind, and decided to stay outside for another few minutes. The weather was still inviting. Besides, he had no obligations. He didn't know why, but the situation reminded him of his pal, Burnell, from basic training.

"When there's food, you eat it." They were always so hungry. It didn't matter what they'd been serving.

Simon settled back into his seat and enjoyed the relaxing day.

Timothy stared through the high-powered binoculars he'd gotten from Ragnar. He was half a mile away, but he was staring at Simon Orlov. Timothy had planted the Claymore in the courtyard of the assisted living facility. Ragnar had been able to hook up a radio receiver, so Timothy could make a phone call and ignite the device. Now that the damn cat was gone, Timothy could get down to business.

Timothy was a bastard alright, but he wasn't a monster.

Cleon got out of his car, navigated through the parking lot, and made it to the edge of the courtyard. Simon Orlov was exactly where he was supposed to be, relaxing under the tree near the benches. Cleon had a rough idea of a plan, but he knew he'd have to improvise. There were still parameters of certain things that were off limits, but at this point, he knew he had some room to maneuver.

Slowly, he approached. Cleon didn't have any formal training. Most of his technique relied on brute force, and along the way he'd picked up combinations from some knowledgeable friends.

Cleon wore a knuckleduster belt buckle, which he had clandestinely slipped on his fingers when he got within one hundred feet of Orlov ... before an explosion occurred.

Dirt kicked up along the racetrack as Chastity in Bloom crossed the finish line. It wasn't a race, just the end of a workout. Cleon knew he was pushing it standing by the finish line as he hadn't healed completely, but he'd graduated from a walker to a cane, so why not celebrate the small victories?

"What do you think?"

Barry Fitz-Hume, owner and trainer of Mr. Ham Sandwich and a few of the horse's subsequent offspring, had already made a verbal agreement to sell Chastity in Bloom to Cleon, but now that the man was here, they could sign the paperwork and make it official.

"Let's do it."

Chastity's driver took her for another lap as part of a cool down, and Cleon and Barry headed toward the front porch of the house next to the stable. They sat at a table with a pitcher of iced tea, two glasses, and the paperwork. Barry poured them both drinks, and Cleon handed him a manilla envelope with a cashier's check for the transaction.

Both men sat back and appraised Cleon's new purchase as she did another lap around the track. Fitz-Hume wore a straw hat and overalls; he didn't look like one of the greats, but as Cleon had learned, looks could be deceiving.

As for Simon Orlov, even thinking of the man's name caused a flare-up in Cleon's hip. Cleon chewed on an ice cube to try and take his mind off it. However, by the time he'd signed the final page of the contract, the pain in his hip had become a dull throb. It would continue to recede over time.

Fitz-Hume poured them some more iced tea.

The explosion had been caused from someone

A BUREAUCRATIC DESIRE FOR REVENGE

detonating a Claymore mine. Detectives were continuing to investigate, but no one had yet been charged. Instead, the incident served as a catalyst for various departments to review the facility for impropriety. The district attorney was still building a case against the director, Martin Chalmers, that included embezzlement and racketeering.

Upon conferring his payment, Sistrunk had told Cleon that Sistrunk had become a person of interest when analysts had gone through Chalmers' records. Sistrunk said he would most likely cut a deal with the DA about Chalmers, probably also connect them to Timothy Jacobs, but Sistrunk would leave Cleon out of it.

The Claymore had misfired, so only half the payload had been dispersed. The tree and had been destroyed, but except for his hearing, Simon Orlov was unscathed. Cleon sipped some more of his iced tea. The misfire had sent a few projectiles his way, but in the grand scheme of things, it could have been worse.

One day, The Grim Reaper would come after Simon Orlov, and Death was undefeated. Orlov would probably have a send-off with full military honors at Arlington National Cemetery. Maybe he'd be buried near Joe Louis and Lee Marvin. Until then, though, Cleon had some more important things to think about—like getting Chastity in Bloom ready for the races at Oxen Hill.

ABOUT THE AUTHOR

Andrew Davie has worked in theater, finance, and education. He taught English in Macau on a Fulbright Grant, at the university level in New York and Hong Kong, and at the middle/high school level in Virginia. Currently, he's pursuing his Clinical Mental Health Counseling Degree, and has survived a ruptured brain aneurysm and subarachnoid hemorrhage.

He has published short stories in various places, a memoir and addendum, and crime fiction books with All Due Respect, Close to the Bone, Alien Buddha Press, and Next Chapter. He also co-hosts a music review show called Happy Hour with Heather and Guest.

To learn more about Andrew Davie and discover more Next Chapter authors, visit our website at www.nextchapter.pub.

A Bureaucratic Desire For Revenge
ISBN: 978-4-82415-817-8
Mass Market

Published by
Next Chapter
2-5-6 SANNO
SANNO BRIDGE
143-0023 Ota-Ku, Tokyo
+818035793528

29th November 2022

www.ingramcontent.com/pod-product-compliance
Lightning Source LLC
LaVergne TN
LVHW032012070526
838202LV00059B/6407